Book Cover Illustration by Lana @redhead_trickster

Book Cover Design by Catrina Bell

Illustrations by Brina Boyle @artbybrina, Daniel Toro @dannotc_graphics, YArtxr @ylpha_artxr, and Sali's Illustrations @salisillustrations.

Editing by Owl Eyes Proofs and Edits

First edition 2023

To my husband,
the love of my life.
You light my fire.

LUCY LIMÓN

HOLIDAYS ABLAZE

HORNED UP FOR THE HOLIDAYS
a Winter Bliss Romance

Chapter 1
Sofia

I'm hiking along the snowy mountain, scanning for fall-en trees when a tremble moves through the air, shim-mying the snow from the overhead branches. It lands in soft splats around me. Ears perking, I pick up the low rumble of an engine growing louder, getting closer, but how? The road is closed. No one can get up here. A second later, a helicopter bobs over the tree line. Its spinning blades chop the air as it speeds my way, then comes to a stop. It hovers only meters away.

They're lost. The Emberlight Resort is the next peak over on Mount BZB, a luxury destination with a five-star hotel, powdery ski slopes, a flashy casino, and most importantly, a helipad. This mountain, Mount Winter Bliss, has none of that. I'd try waving them east, but I doubt they can see me through the dense trees.

I'm about to dismiss the helicopter and its directionally challenged pilot when a person falls out the side. *¡Dios mío!* I gasp, my hand clamping over my mouth. Through the trees, I see the body hit the frozen lake. An ominous thud shudders across the snowy landscape. I don't know if it's real or imagined, but I swear I hear the crunch of bones on impact.

My next thought? I hope it's Ryan.

Morbid, I know, and if I were a better person, I'd immediately dismiss it. But I hold on to the thought, breathing in the dark joy and sweet catharsis of imagining the man who destroyed my future falling to his death. I suck it in, then exhale and let it go.

Whoever it is, I better go see if they're alive. The helicopter is a tiny speck on the horizon. I'm guessing they're not coming back for their fallen passenger. I pick up the strap to my firewood-laden sled, cherry red with silver bells on its nose, and start trudging towards the lake. I'd make better time if I left it, but it's easier to drag a sled to a person than a person to a sled, and there's no way that person is walking away from that fall. They'll need a doctor or a hearse, but all I have is *La Roja*, my trusty sled.

It's not Ryan.

That much is obvious before I reach the edge of the frozen shore. There's no reason it would be, but I'm mildly disappointed, nonetheless. How do I know? Ryan is not a demon (just a fucking asshole), and the man lying flat on his back is one. His pronounced horns are an ombre of burnt orange to golden-yellow, jutting out from his hairline and curving halfway back over his head.

A tender concern blooms in my chest, and it draws me across the frozen lake, solid this time of year. I imagine myself laying gentle hands on him, whispering that he's not alone, that I'm here, and I'll take care of him. It's entirely misguided. These feelings have nothing to do with the man on the ice and everything to do with a childhood memory of the demon who pulled me from a fire I'd started. For reasons that are no great psychological mystery, I've had a soft spot for demons ever since, which is lucky for this one since there's not another living soul around for miles. I'm all the rescue this fallen angel can hope for.

My sled and I come to a stop at his head. He's unconscious but breathing. I'm relieved to see his chest moving and puffs of steamy air coming out of his nose. Demons are made of sturdy stuff, and a fall that might kill a frail human, say Ryan, for example, is survivable for demonkind. Looking straight down, I take in his angular features, deep-set eyes, full lips, neatly manicured eyebrows and beard. He's adorned with small accents of glinting gold, a set of double studs over his right eyebrow and cuffs on his ears. I'd guess he's around my age, late twenties or early thirties, with burgundy skin and hair that's the same color but darker, almost black. This close, I can see the texture of his horns, a pattern of spiraling ridges that I imagine would feel like a seashell if I reached out and touched one. The play of his orangy-golden horns against his dark red features is stunning, and for a moment, I'm breathless. He's possibly the most beautiful man, demon or otherwise, I've ever seen. Who in their right mind would leave him behind?

He groans.

"Don't move," I say. I have zero medical background. I know the Heimlich maneuver and that's it, but I'm a hundred percent sure I've heard people on TV tell injured people not to move. Although, if he doesn't move, I'm not sure how I'll get him on my sled. His eyes open, and I tug down my left sleeve, wishing I'd remembered my gloves. I pull my hoodie strings to tighten the hood around my face, adjusting the left side so that more of my cheek is covered. I'm not usually self-conscious about my burns, but after the fallout with Ryan, I don't know. I'm a little more wary than I used to be.

I'm itching to ask him about the helicopter but now doesn't feel like the time. "Try sitting up slowly," I say, once again sounding like well-scripted TV. Kneeling on the ice, I offer him gentle assistance by sliding one hand behind his back and holding out my other. He takes it. His fingers close over mine with a firm, warm grip that hums against my palm like a circuit connecting. "Does anything feel broken?"

I ask in a steady yet concerned voice, admiring my own bedside manner. Maybe I have a calling as a nurse. I am in need of a career change. So, it's something to think about.

I wonder if he's a criminal. Normal people don't get dropped out of helicopters. As his nurse, I'd be obligated to tend to this beautiful outlaw regardless, and that's exactly what I mean to do.

"Who the fuck are you?" He jerks his hand away, breaking our connection, and his black eyes snap up to glare at me. Rude. The nurse illusion shatters, and I bristle at his question. *Who the fuck am I?*

"I'm Sofia Maria Moreno, and it's my lake you just landed on. Who the fuck are you?" And now he knows that if he gets salty with me, I'm going to get salty right back.

"It's kind of tiny for a lake," he snorts as he looks around, gauging the distance from one edge to the other, which, to be fair, is not very far. His voice is deep and grumbly. "Not exactly a prized feature worth bragging about." Again, very rude, and I have to clamp my mouth shut to avoid snapping at him. In my kitchen, snarky attitudes were never tolerated, but I don't run a kitchen anymore, and he doesn't work for me.

"It's a stock pond, and it's exactly the right size for one," I say, crossing my arms.

"Then don't call it a lake," he says. And now he's eyeing me up and down, and though I try not to, I squirm under his gaze. It must be the black eyes. They're intense, very—penetrating. His brows pinch, and the edge of his lip curls downward into a grimace. "Mother Darkness," he curses under his breath. "What are you wearing?"

I look down at my triple layer of flannel plaid shirts poking out from under my hoodie with my leather duster jacket over the top of it. It's old and worn and belonged to my grandfather. Only now do I notice the demon's clothes. He's wearing an expensive-looking wool sweater fitted to his lean torso. His shoes look expensive, too, probably Italian leather, and his pants. Well, fuck if I know what they're made of. I'm not a clothes horse, but that's obviously some tailoring wizardry in the inseam that's showing off his package.

So, he's more like Ryan than I gave him credit for, another rich asshole. Great. Merry Christmas to me. I give him a withering look and rise to my feet.

He stands up, too, and he's not even a full head taller than me if I don't count his horns, which makes him short for a demon. Ha. He rubs the back of his head. But other than that, I don't see any blood or protruding bones. I guess he's fine.

"Are you homeless?" he asks. Looking around again, his black eyes take in the fact that there are only woods around, nothing else. At least he has the decency to sound confused and not disgusted.

"No," I snort, but the real answer is more complicated than that. I recently gave up my apartment, and everything

I own is in boxes, stashed in a cabin, but that doesn't make me homeless. Does it? *Shit, am I homeless?* This property belongs to my family, which means technically, I own something like one-sixteenth of ten acres. That's not nothing.

"I'm staying at my family's cabin," I say, not adding that it's a temporary situation, just until I figure something else out. Then, out of an abundance of generosity, and I suppose the holiday spirit since it is almost Christmas, I offer the stranger my hospitality. "If you need a place to stay, the couch folds out."

"Folds out to what?" His brows are knitted again, and the double stud piercings over his right brow rise like a question mark. Of course this Ryan-esque demon, *el demonio Ryan*, doesn't know what a fold-out couch is.

"I'm offering you a place to sleep," I say with a sigh. "But feel free to burrow into the snow at nightfall if you prefer. I'm sure you'll be toasty warm."

"I won't be here at nightfall. I'm going back to my hotel at the resort."

"Good luck with that," I say, picking up the sled strap so that *La Roja* and I can be on our way.

"Wait!" He catches up to me quickly. "I need a car. Lend me yours, and I'll return it with interest."

"With interest?" I snort. "What does that even mean?"

"It's an opening offer. I'm trying to strike a bargain with you," he says, as if that should have been obvious.

"I don't own a car," I say. I gave it up along with the apartment and for the same reason. Because once your dreams are dead, and your future is smashed to smithereens, things like apartments and cars don't really matter much anymore. Plus, I couldn't afford to keep them.

"Whatever modest mode of transportation you do have access to then. Tell me what it'll cost me to borrow it." He pats his pockets as if taking stock of what's on him. "My phone!" He sucks in a horrified breath and comes to an abrupt stop. I keep moving. I've spotted a fallen tree, and *La Roja* is far from full. I won't be heading back to the cabin until she is.

"My phone! Did you see it?" He's panicking. I hear him run back to the lake, sorry, *pond*, I assume to look for his phone.

I can hear his cries of dismay as he traipses in circles in the distance. I get out my ax and walk around the fallen tree. The inside is hollowed out, and a very particular shape catches my eye. Morels in winter? It's a miracle! Although miracles do happen when one lives on an active volcano. The wild edibles I've foraged on the slopes of Mount Winter Bliss are mind-blowingly good. I drop to my knees and scoot and squeeze my way inside the fallen log, trying to get at the mushrooms.

"Is that where you live?" Ryan-demon is back.

"Does this look like a cabin?" I shout, my voice echoing inside the log. He doesn't answer. "I'm collecting mushrooms," I say as I roll my eyes. He can't see me. So, it's for my own benefit.

"I see," he sounds disturbed.

"Morels! They're a delicacy!" I don't know why I'm bothering to explain anything to him. When I resurface with my haul, he avoids looking at me. "Did you find your phone?" I ask. I don't bother to tell him that cell service is shit up here. His phone won't do him any good unless he's willing to make the two-hour hike out to Frostwing Lookout.

"No," he answers, and his eyes flash with irritation. "May I use yours?" He asks through gritted teeth.

I hold the morels up to my nose and sniff. "There's no cell service up here," I say as my eyes flutter closed, and my plans for dinner start to rework themselves in my head. Earthy. I'll have to make some tweaks to balance out the flavor. Then there's the texture to consider. I imagine the feel of sauteed morels under my teeth, soft with a bit of chew.

"What are you doing?" Ryan-demon demands to know, but he doesn't wait for my answer. "Look, I don't have anything on me to offer as payment up front, but given your—circumstances, I'd say it's in your best interest to help me get back to my hotel. You have my word. I'll make it worth your while."

I open my eyes and raise an eyebrow at him. "Breaking your own rules, aren't you? I didn't think demons dealt in maybes and vagaries."

"Don't believe every children's rhyme you hear," he says gruffly. "If my hotel hasn't been ransacked, I can pay you in cash as soon as we get there. If it has—" His teeth grind together, "I'll make good another way. I swear." I note the beads of sweat on his forehead, probably from the panicked circles he just ran. But they could also be signs of desperation. He really wants to get back to his hotel.

"I do have my sister's car," I say, and he brightens. She lent it to me for my move up to the cabin, my retreat from the world, and its many disappointments. "But there's only one road down the mountain, and it's blocked. An avalanche buried it ten feet deep a few hours ago. Until the road crew clears it, there's no way off the mountain."

He stares at me, stunned. I offer my cabin to him again, although I don't know why I bother. "You're lying." His eyes narrow. "You run some sort of earthy, wilderness, subsistence living, eco-tourism kind of place, don't you? And you want me to rent it, that's what this is. You're trapping me here. For what? A rental fee and a five-star review? I'll give you both. Just get me down the mountain today. Now!"

This demon is an idiot, I note with mild amusement and a touch of pique at his continued disdain for mountain-side living. I'm not exactly a permanent resident, but I spend a few weeks up here every year, and it's nothing to look down your nose at. This mountain is a very special place for those with enough sense to appreciate it. I wouldn't accuse this demon of having either, not sense nor an abundance of appreciation.

"A rental fee? Does that mean you're in a position to pay for your stay?" I ask, and that gets a very satisfying reaction. He glowers at me. I've already offered to take him in twice. If he's going to be an ass, free is off the table.

"I can't pay now. I don't have my wallet," he grumbles.

"Well then, it sounds like we'll have to work out some kind of bargain after all. I have room and board to provide, and you have nothing." He pulls back, affronted by a statement of fact. If I were running a restaurant, he'd be on dishes. But that's not the situation. "Chores it is. I'll give you tasks to earn your keep, starting with this." I hand him the ax. "I need a stack of long logs, six feet each. Start chopping. We'll head back to the cabin when the sled is full." I hold up my hand to show the stacked height of my expectations.

"You can't be serious." He sneers at the ax in his hands.

"Oh, I'm very serious, Ryan," I say with an icy glare as my chest puffs. He thinks he can question me in my own kitchen, er, woods? "My woods, my rules. Take it or take a hike." There's iron in my voice, and he hates it. I can tell by the flashes in his eyes. Sparks like those flew my way every time a new *pinche* hotshot chef swaggered into my kitchen, dribbling their ego-swollen *cojones* between their legs. Hot shits always think they deserve respect they haven't earned. But when I lock horns, I always win.

"The name is Samite." He corrects me, but he turns and swings the ax. I smile to myself. We've struck a deal.

Chapter 2
Samite

I stare daggers into the back of the walking potato sack of a human being ahead of me. I've been made her indentured servant, forced into menial labor by a snippy vagabond. Of all the people in the world, why did she have to be the one to find me? It's not like I needed more proof that my string of bad luck continues unbroken.

The deal I came to town for fell through last night at the last second. We'd shaken and were about to sign, but then my luck went south, and my would-be partner walked. If only I'd gone back to my hotel room, I might have snipped that string. But no, I headed to the bar and overstayed until my Brimstone Bourbon-sodden brain decided it was time to hit up the casino. Gambling? That's not me.

I'm not that kind of demon.

I'm the type to hedge my bets and wait for the upper hand. Uncalculated risks are for amateurs and imbeciles who don't know how to bide their time and strike while the iron is hot. My blood tingles just thinking about that sublime moment when a bargain is struck highly in my favor. I swear by Mother Darkness, there is nothing better. But given my string of recent luck, it's been a while since I've felt that glow and ridden that high. Last night's deal was supposed to change that.

Instead, I spent the night grumbling and throwing around chips like I was trying to make myself a target. I was practically daring those hairy-knuckled thugs to abduct me. I should have been more careful. Of course, thieves would be circling a casino during the busy holiday season, and of course they'd target wealthy demons. But that's where my respect for their methods ends. There is absolutely no class in using such obvious threats of violence. Dangling me from a helicopter? I snort in disgust. Pathetic. If you can't con your opponent, outwit or outmaneuver them, then you don't deserve their money. Those clowns certainly didn't earn mine. But until I get back to my hotel, there's no way to know if they got their fleshy paws on it.

If it's gone, I'm ruined.

Meanwhile, this heartless hermit refuses to help. She sneered at my offer of fair financial compensation in exchange for her assistance and instead tasked me with chopping wood and hauling it on a sleigh with real-life jingle bells on it! I may be the demon, but she's the monster.

"This is it." She comes to a stop ahead of me. We're still in the middle of nowhere. There's nothing around to see except for a ten-foot, debris-packed wall of snow. So, what the hell is she talking about?

"This is what?" I growl. Instead of answering me, she kicks at a wooden post sticking out of the snow and keeps kicking it until the road sign attached to it appears. Satisfied, she steps back and waves for me to have a look. "Last Hour Road," I read. "Is that supposed to mean something to me?"

"It's the road down the mountain. The only road. And like I said, it's impassible." She waves both arms at the snow wall like she's presenting a gameshow prize. "You sounded doubtful, so I took us on a little detour to give you some proof." She grins out from the drawstring hoodie that fits like a scrunchy around her face. It's the single worst fashion choice I've ever witnessed. I barely know what this woman looks like because I can't see past the awful face scrunchy or the leather potato sack of a jacket. My eyes literally sting just looking at her. I turn away and eye her so-called proof that I'm stranded on this mountain.

I glance sideways and catch the merry glint in her eye. If I was pissed before, I'm edged towards furious now. She thinks this is funny. She's taking pleasure in my misfortune. "How big of a detour?" I ask through gritted teeth. I'm hauling a sleigh weighted down with logs — a massive, back-breaking load of logs — while simultaneously sweating and gathering icicles on my balls. And she's taken us on a detour? The nerve of this woman!

She shrugs. "Maybe a mile out of our way. But don't worry, the cabin isn't far. We'll be there in half an hour, less if you pick up the pace. Come along, Samite," she says, and turning around, she retraces our steps, heading back the way we came.

Sweet Mother Below. I cringe at the sound of my name coming from her mouth. I should have let her keep calling me Ryan.

⁂

We arrive at a wooden cabin that has all the charm of a kid's drawing made life-size. Uninspired and unoriginal. I scan the surroundings, keeping an eye out for a satellite dish, phone lines, an old school antenna, any evidence of a connection to the outside world. I see nothing, but it doesn't mean she's being truthful about how cut off we are. The better the technology, the less it announces itself. The cell booster in my car is the size of a breath mint.

She shows me where to leave the sled, and we clomp up the porch stairs with me a step behind her. There's a holly wreath on the door, because of course there is, and I'm guessing a trimmed tree awaits us inside.

She knocks the snow off her boots before opening the door and motioning me inside. *"Pásale,"* she says with a tight-lipped smile that I don't mistake for a warm welcome. I dip my head to keep my horns from scraping the door-frame, and as soon as I'm inside, I see that I'm right. A fir tree topped with a miniature angel, a human holiday cliché. There are also ropes of pom-pom garland hanging over the fireplace, a hazard, and red and green striped blankets piled on the couch, an eyesore.

I furtively scan the walls. No phone, no cable jacks, no digital panels nor blinking power lights of any kind.

"Quaint," I say as she passes me and heads to the kitchen. Ah, now there is a fine-looking room. I follow her, admiration drawing me into the space. My eyes need this, something worthwhile to look at. There is a truly massive wood hearth made of brick and iron. It's obviously well used and well cared for, no caked soot. The island counter is almost grand in scale and made of oiled and sanded butcher block. The hanging pots and pans are weighty cast iron and welded stainless steel. No flimsy aluminum here. This kitchen may have an old-world feel, but it's not quaint. It's—impressive, especially given the cabin it has the misfortune to exist in.

I glance at her, a well-deserved compliment on the tip of my tongue, when she strips her ancient leather duster jacket, revealing a brown hoodie, and I'm stunned into silence. There's a red-nosed Rudolph on the front. It's equal parts ridiculous and hideous. I squeeze my fists at my side, fighting the urge to reach out and burn it right off her. I'd be doing her and the world a favor.

Thank the Dark Mother Below, I don't have to look at it long. She unzips it and the face scrunchy hood comes off with it too.

Uh-oh. My stomach drops. Without the hood to hide them, there are obvious burn marks across her neck and cheek. Glancing down, I notice them on her left hand too. Fuck. I've met fire-scarred humans before, and they always hate demons. No wonder she's stonewalling and refusing to help me get off this mountain. I'm surprised she invited me into her home. Maybe she thinks she can murder me. Fat chance.

I look away, but a flicker of light catches the corner of my eye and draws my attention back to her. She shakes out her black, wavy, shiny hair. It's surprisingly luxurious for a home-spun, backwoods woman. I imagined her having a rat's nest under that hood or a hatchet job haircut, but no. Her hair is lovely. Hmph.

She continues to strip one plaid shirt after another, three in total, revealing smooth, rich brown skin and a clingy white t-shirt. I swallow a noise of surprise. She is considerably less potato shaped than I'd originally assumed, but I don't need to be caught ogling a woman who already has the upper hand. It's bad business. I turn my back to her.

"I need a shower," I say over my shoulder. I smell of dry sweat and last night's booze mixed with outdoor odors. I'm itching to scrub it off.

"That'll cost extra. How about laundry? A load of towels for a shower?" she asks, and I accept her terms. Shoving a few towels into a washing machine won't kill me.

"Great. You can have a shower after I've had mine. Fair warning, the water heater tank is small. So, you'll want to be quick." She tries to walk past me, but it's easy to block her, one of the benefits of a small space.

"I hate cold showers. Let me go first." Scalding hot showers are what I like. At home, I have a steam jet shower with a lava-water setting. No exaggeration, it's the absolute best thing in my life. I won't be getting anything close to that here since humans prefer a disturbing lukewarm temperature, barely tolerable, but a cold shower? I can't. I won't.

She puffs her chest, and I can't help but glance down, and it's a good thing I do. Her nipples harden beneath her shirt, peeking through at me. I stifle my grin, along with the urge to bid them hello. When friendly nipples salute, I like to salute back.

"I go first," she says in that steely, unbending tone of hers. I didn't care for it out in the woods, but now, when I'm looking right at her tits, the sound of it hits a little differently. I feel a familiar tug in my pants.

"I could join you," I say, a genuine offer but also a test, and sure enough, those friendly little tips get harder, a reaction that's all too easy to read under her thin shirt.

"Absolutely not," she says, but nipples don't lie. They like me, which means at least part of her likes the idea. I can barely keep the grin off my face as I continue eyeing her tits, round and full. I'd really like to bite one and give the other a bouncy little squeeze. I take my time imagining it. She doesn't hate that I'm looking at her. And I don't hate the view or the slight shift in the power balance. In fact, I'm thrilled. It seems my luck might finally be changing.

I step aside. "Be quick, or I'm coming in." I lean in close and catch the taste of excitement in the air. Demons are supernaturally attuned to arousal and fear, a boon in every situation, but especially one like this. She's mildly aroused and not at all afraid. I can work with that. She doesn't have to like demons to be seduced by one. And if it'll get me off this gods-forsaken mountain, I'll do whatever I have to. Happily.

I lean against the wall and listen as the water turns on. I note the unhurried sounds of her taking her sweet time while I picture the stream of precious hot water running straight down the drain. I growl at the door before it dawns on me that she's being slow on purpose. My cock twitches, tugging at my pants once more.

Is she inviting me in? No. She's daring me.

"If you think I'm bluffing, you're sorely mistaken," I yell through the door. "Five minutes and I'm stripping naked and entering your shower!" It's an excellent play. Either way, whether she hurries or takes her time, I win. I prowl the hallway, waiting to see what she'll do.

Four minutes later, she steps out of the bathroom wrapped in a fluffy green robe with a towel piled on her head. "It's your turn," she says primly. "The towels will be waiting for you on the back porch in the basin. Once you've hand washed them, hang them on the clothesline to dry." She disappears behind the only other door leading off the hallway, her bedroom, I assume.

"You can't be serious! There's no washing machine?" I shout after her. She doesn't answer. What the fuck? I grumble as I strip out of my clothes, taking just a second to fold them neatly before I jump in the shower. I don't have my obsidian body scrub or my lathering night-bloom bar, and without my phone, there's no hope of contracting a delivery service to air drop me a care package. Cost be damned, I'd happily pay through the teeth for either of those items right now.

The dribbling water goes from warm to shivery in well under five minutes. So, I'm more cold than clean when I jump out. I'm naked, dripping onto the tiniest bathmat I've ever seen. It's soaked through and squishes under my toes. I have no towel, no razor, no hair products, and no toothbrush. I'm already devolving into an ungroomed mountain man. I snort, and the breath steals too much air from my body; my chest deflates, and my shoulders slump. I want to be home in my own bathroom, surrounded by the beautiful, hand-selected finishes, every texture, color, and scent exactly to my liking.

Instead, I'm here.

Something red catches my eye. Hanging on the back of the door is a robe. I know it wasn't there earlier. Did she leave it for me? I stare at it, finding it hard to believe, but she's the only one here, so it has to be from her.

Cautiously, I take the robe and put it on. My clothes stink, but this is clean and so soft, I groan as it slides over my skin. I'm wrapped in an ethereal, floating comfort. My hands slip into the front pockets, and I pull out two handfuls of toiletries, including a plastic toothbrush, a disposable razor, and a tiny tube of night-bloom scented oil for beard, mane, and horns. The same scent I use at home.

I glance at the door, then back at the items in my hand. It's a bargain. It has to be. An offer made at just the right moment, when I am in need and therefore most susceptible to temptation. Clever. And opportunistic. This human just might have a shine for devilry, I note with a begrudging twinge of admiration. It's something I'll have to keep in mind. For now, I have a choice to make. If I accept these small luxuries, I'll be able to groom myself properly. But I'll be further indebted to a woman who has already tricked me with the towels. I roll the bottle of night-bloom oil in my hand, considering it. I'll owe her. And there's no telling what she'll ask of me, I think as I recall her perky, friendly nipples.

So be it.

I set out my haul of fun-sized toiletries on the rickety counter and get to work de-mountain-manning myself.

Chapter 3
Sofia

Fire is my canvas and my muse—a force that breathes life into my hungry soul and sets my imagination ablaze. I smooth the front of my chef's jacket. It's time to start dinner.

My preparations begin with the stacking of logs. Today, I'm working with oak and cherry. Despite the joint ownership of the cabin, the kitchen is mine. Years ago, I tore out the old appliances, keeping only my grandmother's *comal* for cooking the perfect tortilla. I built this hearth, brick by brick, until it was waist height and an arm and a half deep, and it's been mine to care for and clean ever since. I grab the first log, its rough bark scraping against my palm as I place it in the cast iron grate.

Always know how and when you'll stop a fire before you start it.□

The words ring like a gong in my head, recalling words of wisdom passed to me by the demon who pulled me from the burning shed all those years ago. I started the fire that almost killed me, and to this day, I hear him every time I touch something I intend to burn. With a glance behind me, I confirm the fire extinguisher is close by. My plan is to let these logs burn down to cooking coals, but should I need it, I have the extinguisher.

Once the logs are stacked, I crumple sheets of paper and shove the wads under the grate. The pages come from a cardboard box that contains the scraps of my dreams. My earliest notes are in there, as are the floor plans and the concept drawings I sketched for an entirely open-flame kitchen restaurant. But what I'm burning today aren't drawings. These pages are from the contract Ryan and I signed, a binding agreement that, in the end, bound me more than him. He was supposed to be my financial backer, yet somehow, when he walked away halfway through renovations, I was the one on the hook for a broken lease and a slew of unpaid bills.

I click the lighter, *click, click,* just to test it before I unclip my kitchen timer from my jacket and set it for ten minutes. An extra safeguard. I've only ever been mesmerized by fire the one time, but the feel of it is sharp and clear in my mind. I was so completely lost and enthralled by my little bucket fire that it grew into a shed fire without my noticing until my sleeve caught.

Click. I light the paper, and as I watch the flames catch, I feel a similar spark within me. It warms my skin. The first tendrils of delicate smoke reach my nostrils, and I inhale the familiar aroma of danger and fascination.

"I smell fire." An unexpected voice, dark and smooth, startles me, and I let out a surprised warble I'm not proud of and spin around. I'd forgotten about my unwelcome guest. Samite is standing in my kitchen, horns shined up with oil, his hair and beard neatly groomed. He's wearing the red robe I left for him, if only just. The belt is so loosely tied that the opening gapes at me. I gape back as warmth trickles down the center of my body.

His torso, to borrow a phrase, is a prized feature worthy of bragging about. Without thinking, I suck in a breath and let out a low whistle. The smooth plane of his abdomen is an alluring texture, and my tongue darts against the back of my teeth, imagining what a nice, long lick would feel like.

"What are you burning besides holes in my chest?" He's being smug, and the spell is broken. I come to, grateful for the snap back to reality. He may be a feast for the senses but given that there's no escape for either of us for the foresee-able future, it's probably best not to indulge.

"I'm starting on dinner," I say and turn back to the hearth. I crumple a few more wads of paper and shove them, one by one, under the grate.

"Good, I'm famished," he says, and I feel the tickle of his breath on my hair. He's come up behind me, close enough to look over my shoulder. "Do you have anything I could nibble on while I wait?" I feel his warmth pass to me, and the magnetic pull that unerringly draws me to fire, shifts direction, rocking me back on my heels. I bump against him, the barest of touches, but it sizzles over my skin all the way down to my toes. It's—unnerving.

"You have towels to wash," I say, but there's a thin quaver in my voice that robs it of my usual firmness.

"I thought I might work off the robe and toiletries first. I've just had a very interesting idea of how I'd like to repay you. Would you like to hear it?" His voice is thick with promise and oh so close to that sensitive spot on my neck. If I tilt my head, would he lick me? Bite me? My pulse spikes.

I could let him take a nibble. He's asking so nicely, after all. I'm about to tilt my head, but he moves first, shifting to whisper into my other ear, "I have a generous first offer, but you should know, anything you want is on the table." I'm suddenly hyper-aware of my scarred cheek, and a cold shiver runs over my skin as I recall the look on Ryan's face the last time I saw him, a mix of confusion and revulsion.

I step sideways and turn to face Samite, opening a gap between us. "Do you have any dietary restrictions?" I ask.

He gives me a puzzled but thoroughly intrigued look. He misunderstands me.

"Allergies or aversions to specific foods," I clarify.

"I know what dietary restrictions are," he says with a bemused smile that tells me he's still puzzling out where I'm going with this.

"I have a six-course tasting menu planned, and I need to know if there's anything you don't eat."

"Virgin pussy. I don't eat it." He says, resting a hip against the butcher block island. "Too high in sodium."

My lip trembles as I fight back a smile. I fail, and I smile for a half second before I wrestle it off my face and give a perfunctory food service industry nod. "I'll make a note and have your dinner adjusted accordingly."

"I'm very adventurous otherwise. Please make a note of that as well. Tell the chef I'd rather she not be too gentle. My mouth is hers to do with as she pleases."

"Also noted." I'm still clamping down hard on a smile. It's just tawdry, flirty banter, so why do I like it so much? I do love an adventurous eater, for one. I'd pegged him for picky, and I'm relieved to be wrong. That would have ruined my whole menu, but now my mind is churning, and excitement is bubbling. Adventurous, hmm? Let's test that, shall we?

I grab my leather knife roll from under the counter and unroll it across the butcher block, selecting my eight-inch blade. Time to start chopping. I make quick work of the alliums: shallot minced, red onion diced, leeks chopped.

They get scooped into three separate bowls and are ready for later use.

Samite makes a noise, and I look up. Knife work, like fire, has a way of absorbing my attention. I'd nearly forgotten him again.

"The jacket." He nods at me. "It's not just another poor fashion choice, is it? You're an actual chef." Poor fashion choice? Rude.

"Towels," I say, steely and firm. My voice is back.

"Yes, Chef." I've heard the phrase a hundred times a night in a professional kitchen, but when Samite says it, I blush. His voice is silky and low, and he draws out the two words like he's licking them in naughty ways.

I meet his eyes, so black and smoldering that for a moment, I think I see a wisp of smoke coming from the corners. It's so sexy, it steals my breath. I stop chopping and lay down my knife, my hand trembling. The words "say it again" are right on the tip of my tongue when the kitchen timer goes off.

"What's that?" he asks.

"A task alarm," I say, not looking at him as I fish it out of my pocket and turn it off. "I have a lot of work to do for dinner." I turn around even though everything I need to prep is on the butcher block behind me. What am I doing? I ask myself as I stare into the sink.

"I'll get the towels done," he says, and I hear him exit the back door.

I scraped him off the ice and brought him into my home only a few hours ago without even thinking that the nearest neighbors live miles away. If I was smart, I'd quit ogling him. He's a complete stranger, and though I doubt it, he could be a dangerous criminal. I never ruled that out.

"Holy fuck, it's freezing out here!" he shouts, and I chuckle. He pops his head back through the door. "The washtub has ice floating in it?" The question is in his shrug. He doesn't know what to do.

"Add some hot water from the tap." I nod to the sink. There should be a little hot water left, enough to de-ice the washtub at least.

He brings the tub in, his robe gaping even wider than before, and I try not to look, I really do, but my eyes keep darting to his belt, willing it to slip that last little bit and fall open.

I shake my head and return to my chopping. I'm not ready for this. I haven't been naked in front of someone since Ryan, and the way he looked at me, well, let's just say I never want anyone to look at me that way again.

When the basin is full, Samite carries it back outside. He trips or bumps against something and splash! I hear water hit the deck, followed by a string of curse words, and I chuckle again.

He bursts back through the door, stark naked (a Christmas miracle), and there's practically an audible *click, click, click* as my mind snaps pictures like I'm a paparazzo. But I also have to fight not to laugh. He's radiating outrage and holding his sopping-wet robe at arm's length. "What do I do with this?" For a demon, he can come across as rather helpless.

"Hang it in the bathroom," I say. He stomps off and stomps back a moment later.

"I have nothing to wear."

"I see that," I say, biting back a smile. "Would you like to bargain for some clothing?"

"Terms?" he says, crossing his arms, no hint of his playful flirting from earlier, but he also doesn't shrink from my gaze. In fact, he squares up his hips to face me dead on. Maybe I shouldn't offer a deal and let him stay naked as a special holiday treat to me. I'd take that over cookies, or sugar plums, or marshmallows bobbing in chocolate. I'm nibbling at my lip as I eye his package when he grumbles something, and I snap to. *Damn it.* I've got to stop this.

"I could use another pair of hands in the kitchen. I'll give you a shirt and pants in exchange for your assistance, plus dishes after."

"Why dishes? Shouldn't helping you cook be enough?"

I shake my head no. "For one, you probably won't be much help, and two, you want to eat as well, don't you?"

"Is there a machine?"

"A dishwasher? Nope. You're it." What does it say about me that I enjoy his look of irritated disappointment? He snorts, and it's very hard not to crack a smile, but I manage it.

"Half the dishes," he counter offers, and because the sight of him has me feeling just a teensy bit merry and bright, I accept his terms.

"Half the dishes. Deal."

⁂

He hates the clothes he's wearing, hates them so much that I cannot keep a straight face. I'm delighted by every irritated grumble and scratch. It tickles me in ways I can't explain, and by the time we're done with dinner prep, I'm practically drunk on it.

"Quit laughing," he says for the hundredth time, but he's walking around like a cat with a piece of tape stuck to its back. How am I supposed to not laugh?

"You've really never worn plaid or jeans?" I ask.

"These are not jeans. They're denim-colored burlap. And no, I have never, ever worn plaid. It's hideous, and it chafes as bad as these so-called jeans."

"So salty," I tease. "You're going to over season my dish." I grab the bowl from his hands and tell him to take a seat at the island. "It's time to eat."

When this menu first formed in my mind, it was a highly technical, sophisticated dinner for one, a private symphony for my solitude. But now that I have an audience, something a little more lively and surprising feels right. There's a glow in my chest and a buzz in my ears as I plate the first course. This dinner is no longer a meal. It's a production, *un baile de los sentidos.*

I present Samite his amuse-bouche in a small bronze bowl of glowing red coals with a skewer of quail hearts and thin slices of pickled shallot. Only when the bowl is right under his nose, do I sprinkle a pinch of thyme and flaky salt. The herb hits the coals, and as it burns, it perfumes the air.

I'm gratified by his instinct to inhale deeply. I hate it when a good scent goes to waste.

"Where's yours?" he asks, and I hear him swallow down a mouth full of spit. Another gratifying sight. I've made his mouth water.

"Right here." I place my own bowl of coals on the counter. I strip off my chef jacket and set it aside, and we lock eyes for just a moment before we each pick up our skewer and devour our tiny morsel.

He groans, a deep and throaty sound. "Damn, that's good." His eyes close as he finishes chewing. When they open again, he grins at me, a wolfish grin with the points of his teeth peeking out from behind his lips. "What's next?"

We move from course to course, and there's flame and pageantry at each stage of our progression. Dining is all about enjoyment, and Samite is very good at enjoying himself. He's the perfect audience—attentive, hungry, and eager. When the flames dance, so do his beautiful black eyes.

When his food is ingested, he makes throaty, appreciative noises that sing in my ears. I've cooked my way through many a good dinner service with pride and satisfaction, but this one feels different. My senses are dialed way up. It's like there's a mystery spice floating in the air that both sharpens my pallet and heats my blood.

"It's time for dessert."

He growls in anticipation, and a thrill runs up my spine as I turn back to the fire, ready to perform my last act. Cinnamon tossed on the flames, a melt-away chocolate dome, bits of smoked toffee, raspberry gelee, and a vanilla custard that is so silky and rich that it feels like it's coming on your tongue. It's the texture that always left my guests weak in the knees. I ignore my own dessert as I watch Samite take his first bite. I hold my breath.￿

His lips close over his spoon, wrapping it in a way that makes me a touch jealous. He whimpers a defeated little moan that sends a quivering arrow down into my belly. His eyes close.

"I want to do things to you," he whispers, and because his eyes are still closed, I don't know if he means me or the custard.

"You like it?" I ask. I've become a slut for his compliments.

"Take off your pants." His eyes open. "I want to show you how my tongue feels right now, and I can only think of one way to do it." He smolders at me, tiny flickers of orange glowing at the back of his coal-black eyes. Blood rushes, heating my extremities, and my head swims.

"You want to taste me?" The question comes out of me as a soft whisper, and it floats around the dark cabin lit only by the hearth fire.

"Yes, Chef."

Chapter 4
Samite

There is a particular kind of heat only a cooking fire gives off, and among demons, it's known as Mother's embrace, a flame both gentle and fierce. Its warmth draws you close with the promise of comfort.

Sofia tells me she has a six-course tasting menu in store for us tonight, and as the hearth fire crackles, we prepare food together, or more like she prepares food as I hold bowls and keep out of her way. But as I watch her, I'm struck by the thought that she must feel it, too, the embrace. She's too attuned to the needs of the fire for a human, too tender in her touch, especially for one who has been burned by it.

I sit at the counter when she tells me to, and she serves us dinner. I'm soon enthralled by a performance far beyond any of my expectations, and they've been set by some of the finest restaurants in the world. Her's is a graceful dance, and she performs it just for me. The textures. The flavors. The movements of her body. I devour it all with no wish to stop, even as it becomes painfully clear that I'm being ruined for any other meal. Bite after bite, I am undone.

At least I have the advantage in one important way. No number of chores could pay this off. I could tear down this cabin and build it again, and still, I'd come out ahead. If I am to be ruined, at least I have this satisfaction.□

She moves us on to our last course. The diminished fire is refueled, and she coaxes the flames higher. As they leap, something inside me awakens. The *dancing fire* is an ancestral memory all demons are born with. Sharp and bright in childhood, the image fades over time. Tonight, Sofia Maria Moreno, a name I only now remember her telling me, has coaxed that long-buried memory to life in an exquisite, almost excruciating way. I rub my chest, my thighs. It's too much.

Dessert is served, and my head swims as it melts on my tongue.

"Take off your pants," I tell her, and I don't know what I'll do if she says no. Sweet Mother Below, let her say yes. The more she feeds me, the more I starve. I will make a meal of her to satisfy this hunger.

"You want to taste me?" she asks me softly, and on the air is the faint taste of her want. I am as relieved as I am desperate.

"Yes, Chef." I eat up her every little expression. She blushed last time I said this, but now, her tongue darts out to wet her mouth. Her eyes go heavy lidded.

"Sofia." I roll her name over my tongue as I stand and walk around the island, closing in on her. She follows me with both her eyes and her body, turning with me as I crowd her against the counter and cage her between my arms. Her breath comes quick and heavy, and there's a thick cloud of excitement around her now. So tasty.

I eye the surface over her shoulder. The butcher block is wide open and ready to receive her. In an easy motion, I hoist her atop it. She kicks off her shoes. I undo her pants. She lifts her hips, and I pull them off. I leave her panties on. For now.

"Lay back," I tell her. She makes a little wordless eager noise, and a growl echoes from deep in my belly in response. She stretches out across the butcher block, her legs dangling over the edge with me standing between them.

I run my hands up her thighs, and we both hiss excitedly at the burn. Her flesh against mine should feel cool, my body runs far hotter than a human, but not Sofia. She feels like she has fire in her veins.

My eyes trace the length of her, noting each swell and hollow of her beautiful form, stopping only when I reach the peaks of her breasts. Her nipples point through her t-shirt toward the ceiling. I grin and salute them with a courteous nod before returning my gaze to the delightful view of her spread legs.

"Do you want my mouth on you?" I ask as I tease the edge of her panties with my finger. The red of my skin is a tonal match to the brown of hers, and I wonder if there's demon in her blood somewhere far back along her family tree.

"Yes," she says with a quick nod.

"Then tell me to do it."

"Put your mouth on me," she says, but there's a question in her voice.

"Like you mean it."

"Put your mouth on me. Now." Unbending steel. That is the Sofia I want to devour. I grin, my sharp teeth on full display as I meet her eyes.

"Mmm. Yes, Chef."

"Your eyes," she gasps, lips parting in surprise with a touch of wonder. Not all demons have smoking eyes, and not many would want them. Among demons, it's a tell, and all tells are weaknesses, even between intimate partners. But Sofia shivers with arousal under my hands, and I am glad my eyes smoke for her. I want her to know what she's done to me. I want her to see it, and most of all—I want her to feel it.

I strip off my shirt and toss it aside before lowering my head into the warm valley between her legs. I nip at the delicate flesh of her inner thigh, then bathe it with my tongue. She likes it. Her soft noises and her delicate quivers tell me so. I bite her other thigh just as lightly, only a trace of a red mark left behind, and I lick it away with my tongue.

Her hips lift and her legs fall wider for just a moment before they close around me. They press at my sides, directing me to that sweet spot. As if I don't know where to go, as if my mouth isn't watering hungrily for it. I'm intentionally holding back, engaging my self-restraint. I'll get there, but not yet.

This is only the first course. An amuse-bouche of black lace panties.

I tease my fingers under the lace, swiping deep enough to reach her sensitive places, but I don't linger. The first course is meant to awaken the senses. I knead the flesh around her hips and thighs and dip my fingers, stroking all the fun places hidden beneath that lace.

Next comes my tongue and my teeth. I would not bite such a sensitive place if not for the thin shield to protect her. I place my lips just so, encircling her before I press my teeth in ever so lightly and suck. The textured fabric draws into my mouth, silky yet rough against my tongue with a titillating scratch at the roof of my mouth.

Her body trembles with a gasp and a shudder. "Yes," she breathes, and I harden at the sound. I suck once more before I start to lick, getting rougher as I repeat my strokes. I don't stop until her panties are soaking wet, and then it's time for them to go.

Second course.

I slide the bit of black lace down her legs and toss them aside. "Grab my horns," I say as I lean over her. I throw her thighs over my shoulders, and as soon as I feel the weight of her grip on my horns, I hoist her up off the counter and onto my shoulders to straddle my face. Her head nearly bumps the raftered ceiling. "Hold on tight. You got it?" I ask.

"Yes, keep going," she says. Her voice is raw and breathy, and my blood pumps faster at the sound of it. I will indeed keep going.

With a hand on either of her bare ass cheeks, I lift her up until my tongue finds what it's looking for. It slips along her sensitive folds. The fabric shield is gone, and I groan at the pleasure of my tongue making contact. I lick her over and over, savoring her like a sweet treat. She moans, and her thighs clamp around my neck. I lift her another inch higher, and I thrust my long tongue inside her, wiggling it deep into the wet, scorching heat.

She bucks, and I have to squeeze her ass to keep her from falling off my shoulders. She'll have bruised imprints of my fingers on those cheeks tomorrow.

Keeping her firmly pressed to my face, I continue thrusting my tongue inside her with deep strokes. She uses my horns for leverage and rides up and down in rhythm to my in and out. She cries out each time she bounces against my face, her movements growing more urgent and frantic as she nears her edge. My blood surges in response until I'm painfully erect. My hips roll and strain with every gasping noise she makes. If I don't push her over the edge, I'll come in my pants.

I grind my face against her, shoving my tongue as deep as it'll go, glad for the extra length. I nuzzle my nose into just the right spot to give her some extra friction, and she goes off, singing the song of sweet release for me. Her shuddering walls squeeze my tongue, and her trembling legs kick at my back.

"*Qué bárbaro*," she mumbles on a gusty exhale just before she loses her hold on my horns and falls. I catch her as she goes down with an arm at her hips and a hand behind her head.

I know she thinks she's done, but there's still a final course to come. What's dinner without dessert?

Third course.

I flip her over and lay her on the butcher block, face down, legs dangling. Mmmm... Her naked ass is on display, and I revel in the magnificent sight. Cheeks so round and sweet, with pinpricks of my nails half mooned across them. I take a moment to imagine all the things I'd like to do to her. Then I take one finger and trace a line up from her swollen nub, along her center until my finger arrives at her pucker.

She gasps, and her head pops up off the block. Looking over her shoulder, her eyes lock with mine, and I hold her gaze as I lower my head, my tongue slowly extending. I watch her watch me, noting every little twinge of an expression as I swipe my tongue along the crack of her ass.

Her eyes roll just before her head drops. She presses her forehead into the butcher block, moaning as her cheeks clench. I lick again, and she lets out a couple of panting breaths. I probe at the pucker with the tip of my tongue, and she gasps before unraveling ever so slightly. I don't know if she can come like this, but I'm game to find out.

I spread her cheeks and set a rhythm, licking up and down and in tender circles, probing her just a bit as I massage and knead her flesh. She's flushed a pleasing shade of red and has grown even more tantalizingly hot to the touch. This woman is a delightful torment to my senses. She groans again, and her hips jerk in uncontrolled little spasms that echo in me. I shudder through the string of tremors, willing my knees not to buckle.

"Samite." She says my name, and unlike the last time when I cringed in the woods, this time, my erection strains against the seam of my pants at the sound of it. I want her to say it again. I want her to scream it, and I'm narrowing in on the quickest way to make that happen when she turns to look at me over her shoulder again.

"Put your cock in me. Now."

Looking down, I slide my finger inside her instead, working it in and out, imagining the relief I'd feel if I unzipped my pants and pumped into her this exact same way. I add a second finger, and my hips rock forward as a new wave of tremors moves through me. Holy fuck, I want inside her. "Are you sure? I don't have any protection."

"I'm sure if you are. We can't make a child anyway," she says. That's not entirely true. It's difficult but not impossible, and that's only if she's one hundred percent human. If she's even a fraction demon, it's a much riskier gamble.

"I don't know." My fingers slide out of her, and my arm falls to my side. My heart is still pounding, and my erection is throbbing. I can't remember a time I wanted a woman as much as I want her, but—

I don't gamble.

She lifts herself off the butcher block and slides to her feet. "What's wrong?" she asks in a shaky voice, tensing away from me as if I've suddenly become a threat. She pulls at her white t-shirt, shrinking and twisting until her fire scarred arm is hidden behind her back. I taste the air. There's a sour note of fear. What is she afraid of? A child?

That's my fear. The chance of us making one tonight is small, but not impossible. It's a risk I can't take. "We should stop," I say with more firmness than I feel.

"Of course, whatever you want," she says without looking at me. And before I can say another word, she swipes up her pants from the floor, scoots past me, and disappears down the hallway. I hear the sound of her bedroom door lock, and I slump against the counter.

I'm not entirely sure what just happened, but I'm deeply troubled by the urge that rises in me next. I'm still achingly hard, but for some reason, what I most want to do is knock on her door and apologize. I've done nothing wrong. In fact, I did several things right. So why should I apologize?

I grit my teeth and wrestle against the bubbling feeling. *I'm sorry, Sofia.*

I'm not sorry.

Earlier today, I left my shower with a plan in mind. I was going to seduce her and convince her to help me get back to my hotel. But then she fed me, and if anyone was seduced, it was me. How did that happen? I am the demon.

And yet...

Sofia bargains.

She seduces.

She plays with fire.

This woman is a devil in spirit, and I have been a damn fool in letting down my guard. She is not some hapless human living atop *Mount Deadzone*. She is a skilled opponent. Tomorrow, I'll come up with a new plan that takes that into account. Seducing a seductress is not a workable strategy. I have to be smarter than that.

The longer I'm here, the greater the risk to my personal wealth. All my money, the entirety of my investment egg, could already be gone. But I'm praying to the Dark Mother Below that it's still there. I just need a way off this mountain. There has to be one. I will coax it out of Sofia one way or

another. I am the demon after all, and I will not be out dev-
iled by anyone, least of all this tricky, mountain-dwelling
human.

Chapter 5
Sofia

When I wake up, it takes a moment for me to realize what today is: Christmas Eve. A warm glow fills my heart. Tonight, I'm bringing back my favorite family holiday tradition. Only this year, I'm going big.

As I stretch, I wince. My ass and inner thighs are tender and sore in a very naughty way, and the sensation triggers a flood of memories from last night. I can hear the obscenely loud sounds of Samite licking and sucking on me and feel his horns in my hands, his tongue thrusting deep inside me. I blush red hot all over, with a potent mixture of conflicted emotions.

On the one hand, last night was beyond words. A perfect dinner service, followed by a buffet of carnal delights. It was an erotic fantasy come to life, surreal and unbelievably hot.

On the other hand . . .

I pull out the drawer on my bedside table and reach in. I find the box I'm looking for and shake it. Mostly empty, but there are a few condoms still in there, like I thought. I could have told Samite I had condoms. It might've changed his mind about going further, but I was terrified it wouldn't have. What if he genuinely wanted to stop, and he'd found a polite excuse? If I'd pushed condoms on him, would I have cornered him into telling me the real reason he didn't want to fuck me?

My scars.

What a wonderfully humiliating reprise that could have been. He hasn't even seen the worst of them, only the ripples visible across my neck and forearm. It's my shoulder and side that scared Ryan away. He took one look at the patchwork of pinkish squares left from the skin grafts and bolted. No one before Ryan had ever minded my scars, not enough to say anything about them, anyway.

As soon as my shirt came off, he scrambled out of bed and gave a fake excuse about needing to be somewhere. He stopped answering my calls, and a few weeks later, a bullshit email showed up in my inbox. It said he'd taken his father's advice and conducted a feasibility study. There was a twenty-page report attached full of jargon and charts labeled population density, average household incomes, restaurants per capita, etc. Bullshit.

Maybe the study's conclusion was right. Maybe the little town of Winter Bliss wouldn't have been able to support an upscale restaurant year-round, but I'm certain it had nothing to do with Ryan's decision to bail. He wanted out and so he had the study done, not the other way around. One look at me topless, and it didn't matter how much time and money we'd both sunk into the restaurant. He was gone.

I sigh and drop the condom box back in the drawer, slamming it shut. It's fine. In a day or two, the roads will be clear, and Samite will be gone too. I'll be alone, like I'd planned except I'll have the scorching hot memory of last night to keep me warm. Just thinking about it makes me want to touch myself, but I don't. I'm already anticipating an awkward morning, and I don't think getting myself off to the memory of riding his face will help. Besides, there'll be plenty of time for that after he's gone.

It's Christmas Eve, I remind myself. I have big plans for this evening and a lot of work to do. Up and at 'em.

The dishes are done when I step out into the kitchen. All of them. My fingers hover over my lips as a smile spreads across my face. That wasn't the deal we'd struck. He was only responsible for half of them.

I catch the sound of a light snore and tiptoe over to the couch. Samite is stretched out on the cushions, stark naked, wearing nothing but his gold adornments, ear cuffs, and the double stud piercing above his right brow. My skin heats and tingles at the sight of him even as I chide myself. I should have brought him some pajamas and a blanket and shown him how to pull out the couch before going to bed. I've been a very bad host. And it seems I'm not done being one yet.

Instead of looking away or waking him, I eat him up with my eyes, newly appreciating how beautiful he is in the morning light. My pulse quickens as I bank these images away. More useful memories for when he's gone. The curves of his calves, the strength in his thighs. I linger on his dick, and my breath catches as I remember how badly I wanted it in me last night. I let out a shaky breath and move on to his abdomen. If my eyes had nails, I'd be scratching a trail up his chest to his stunningly perfect face.

His head is adorned with the most beautiful horns I've ever seen on a demon. They're the color of fire, a yellow base that fades to orange at the tip, and they curve from his hairline and loop back over his head, thick and strong. Again, I recall the roughness of their spiraled texture against my palms as I used them as handles to pump myself up and down on his tongue. Heat blooms low in my belly and travels up my chest and neck until the warm glow reaches the crown of my head. I let out another shuddering breath.

"Did you get a good look?" He opens one eye and smirks at me. I glance away, embarrassed he caught me.

"Thank you for doing the dishes," I say, clearing my throat, but there's no hiding the flush of my face. I looked at him for too long.

"There were a lot of them." The couch creaks as he sits up. "You used nearly every dish in there."

"Mm-hm." I agree but don't apologize. Last night's menu was perfection and as my mind wanders towards food, my embarrassment lessens just enough that I can shake it off and shift my focus. I start to reminisce over the menu, recalling the delectable scents, the balance of tastes, and the exquisite textures. There's nothing to apologize for.

"You owe me," he says. My eyes snap to meet his, and I see the challenge flicker in his black eyes. A bargain so early in the morning? I raise an eyebrow, both at him and the unexpected tingle of excitement. This is new for me, but if this is how demons always feel when bargaining, I get the appeal.

"What exactly do you think I owe you?" I ask.

"Coffee?" He asks.

"Fine." I nod, and my excitement flags. It's too small, too easy to agree to. All those dishes for coffee? I'm definitely coming out ahead.

"And eggs."

"Alright." Still leaning in my favor, but there's a flutter in my pulse and a smile teases at my lips. I can tell he's not done.

"Bacon, sausage links, hash browns, a ginger scone with lemon curd, whipped cream on berries."

Ha! I laugh out loud and cross my arms. "Coffee, eggs, toast." My counteroffer.

"Plus bacon."

"Deal."

The exchange is oddly satisfying. We shake, and I feel a rush like I've downed a shot of espresso, and I can't help but wonder if it's because Samite's a demon. It'd probably be rude to ask, so I move off to the kitchen to start breakfast. Naked Samite follows me.

"Aren't you going to get dressed?" I ask.

"No. My clothes are dirty."

"You know where the wash tub is." I jut my chin towards the back porch.

"My sweater is cashmere," he says, as if that's supposed to mean something to me.

"How nice," I say with a blatantly disingenuous smile as I get out the water kettle and start filling it at the sink.

"It needs to soak for at least twenty minutes in cool water before it's hand washed with a very gentle soap, very gentle. It can't be squeezed or spun. It just gets a gentle agitation and then a rinse." He is as adamant as he is naked, and I'm confused, possibly distracted by the closeness of his torso and his exposed everything.

"Why are you telling me this?"

"Because I need your help, obviously." His hands fly up in frustration, but my eyes dart the opposite direction, more attracted to the swing of his dick than the movement of his hands. I get a quick eyeful before I force myself to focus on his face as he continues talking. "I need a safe place to soak my sweater. I'm not leaving it outside for rabid animals and grubby insects to crawl over. And it has to be a mild soap. Your bucket of blue-speckled, industrial-grade powder would absolutely ruin the texture. And once the texture is gone —" he shakes his head before finishing the dark thought, "there is no getting it back."

I miss some of what he's saying as I struggle to keep my eyes above his waistline, but I catch the last of it and pull up straight, ears perking. I've said that exact thing before in my kitchen. 'Once the texture is gone, there's no getting it back.' I've screamed it in frustration. I've fired someone over it.

"The perfect texture is a thing of beauty," I mumble, almost to myself.

"It is." He sounds relieved.

"We'll set up an indoor wash station for you," I say. We find a basin that meets his exacting standards. Then run the tap for five minutes, adjusting the temperature up and down until it's the perfect degree of cool. I find him a travel bottle of baby shampoo which I have to bully him into using.

"It's gentle enough!" I insist.

"How do you know?"

"It's for BAY-BEES. You know, perpetual whiners who cry when they don't get exactly what they want. Sound familiar?"

He sucks in an offended breath. "I am *not* a baby."

"Prove it. Make do with this." I shove the bottle at him. He grumbles and swears under his breath, but he takes it.

While his sweater soaks, I get started on breakfast. Naked Samite offers to light the fire, and with alarm, I watch him do it in the nude. His thighs and dangling bits are so close to the lip of the brick hearth that I feel justified in staring, but he's completely at ease, not worried in the least. I'm the only one on high alert.

He shifts his stance, and now I'm staring at his muscled calves, the toned back of his thighs, and his perfectly shaped ass. If he walked away right now, I'd follow like a rat after the Pied Piper. I bite down on my lip as I imagine grabbing a handful of that ass, maybe smacking it a little. I bet even with all that muscle; it'd have a nice bounce to it.

He pulls a page from my burn box and pauses to look it over. "What's this?"

"Trash," I reply, quickly coming to.

"It looks like a lease agreement," he says and continues reading.

I spring to his side, snatch it out of his hand, wad it up, and shove it under the grate. "It's just trash, good for starting fires."

He's already grabbed another page. "Ryan?" He reads the name aloud and gives me a curious look.

"Also trash," I say through gritted teeth and pluck the page from his fingers. "That's enough." I grab the box and move it to the corner, where I give it a little kick just to make sure it stays put.

I turn back just in time to see him light the fire, not with a match, but with a snap of his fingers. A flame leaps from his hand to the pages. I suck in a breath as they smoke and then catch. Warmth pools between my legs. I wouldn't have said I had a 'thing' before, but now I know I do. It's naked demons starting fires in my kitchen.

He turns to wink at me over his shoulder. "You liked that." The studs over his brow add a cheeky glint. It wasn't a question. Somehow, he knows the answer is yes. It's not just the fire. The points of his teeth, the twist of his lips, the tilt of his head, and the angle of his horns, it's all adding to my new 'thing'. And then there's his shapely, red ass. But that might be a 'thing' of its own.

"It's efficient. No need for a match," I say. "I like efficiency." We both one hundred percent believe me, and I go back to preparing breakfast.

He refuses to hang up his sweater when it's done soaking, worried it will stretch out the material. So, *fine*, we lay it out on towels on the butcher block like he insists. It's annoying and takes up a lot of my workspace. But to be honest, this is the kind of exactness and determination to do things right that I look for when hiring new chefs. I'll take a fastidious pain in the ass over someone sloppy or careless any day.

We eat breakfast together, and it's nice. Far more comfortable than I anticipated when I woke up this morning despite the fact that he's still in the nude.

By late afternoon, his clothes are finally dry, and we can get started on my plans for the evening. We'll be heading out to the lake. I've been cooking and baking, and I've packed a couple of sacks of food and other things to take with us. Tonight is very special, a revival of my favorite holiday tradition. It's been a long time. This is the first Christmas I haven't worked in at least twelve years. At sixteen, I followed my family, parents, siblings, aunts, uncles, and cousins into the hospitality industry. Tourism is the lifeblood of this town. It keeps Winter Bliss a thriving little slice of heaven, and holidays are peak season. Nobody in the industry gets it off.

I dress in layers, many of which are plaid, and I have to hear about it from Samite as soon as I step out of my room. "There are better choices for outdoor attire. All you have to do is go to any store that doesn't have the word 'bin' or 'outlet' in the name. I'll take you to one if you promise to never wear this again." He plucks at my sleeve, then wipes his hand on his jeans.

I roll my eyes. "Are you going to be warm enough without a coat?" It's mid-40s outside, and he only has the single layer of his perfectly textured, not at all ruined by baby shampoo, cashmere sweater.

"I'm a demon. We run hot," he shrugs. "I don't own a coat even though I'd look great in one." Can't argue with that. He looks sexy as sin in clothes, but not nearly as sexy as when he's naked.

Outside, I deliver the bad news that he'll be pulling the sled again, still weighted down with all the logs, and he's outraged. But I promise him we'll go slow so that he doesn't break a sweat. He grumbles the whole way right over the jingling of *La Roja's* silver bells, and it is the grumpiest, bah humbuggy-iest Christmas carol I've ever heard.

"Why are you laughing?" He shouts. He's fallen a couple of meters behind me.

"I'm not!" I shout back, but I can't keep the amusement out of my voice.

We arrive at the lake, sorry *pond*, twenty minutes later. It's not that far from the cabin if you don't take any detours. The sun is low enough to touch the tops of the trees and it casts a cheery, warm glow across the snow.

"This place?" he snorts, and little puffs of warm air shoot out of his nostrils.�

"Yep, this place." I nod. "I'm considering renaming it Samite's Landing. What do you think?" I smile over at him.

He laughs, a really nice laugh, and then shakes his head. "Don't you dare name this miniscule lake after me."

"Aww, you called it a lake." I press my hand over my heart in mock tenderness. "I knew you'd come around."

The first thing we have to do is clear a large area along the shore and build a circular barrier maybe ten feet wide using scavenged stones. Next, we start unloading the sled.

I reach for the first log, and as my hand lands, I hear it again. *Always know how and when you'll stop a fire before you start it.* I go through my mental checklist. This fire is allowed to burn until midnight, no later. The kitchen timer clipped to my jacket is set to warn me twenty minutes before. The fire ring is well away from the tree line and all the brush has been cleared away, even the stuff that was covered in snow. In my pack is a fire blanket and an extinguisher. I also packed two buckets for shoveling snow, just in case. We're good.

"That was a lease for a restaurant space, wasn't it?" Samite asks as, together, we carry the largest log over to our stone circle, one of us on each end. I wince but don't answer. "You were burning it. Is that because your restaurant failed?"

His questions land like a punch right to my gut. I stumble and drop my end of the log. Coming upright, I glare at him.

"What? Most restaurants fail. It's a fair question."

I snort and shake it off and pick up my end of the log.

"Well?" he says. Clearly, he's not taking the hint to drop it.

"It didn't exactly fail. It never got off the ground," I grit out as we lay the log across the middle of the circle. We keep carrying logs over, laying down a nice and stable crisscross base with large gaps for air to circulate.

"People underestimate how complex the industry is. There are a lot of moving parts and even incredibly talented chefs struggle to turn a profit," he says.

"Can we not talk about this?" He's poking at a very tender spot, and I'd rather he stopped.

"It's notoriously competitive."

"I know," I say, wincing at another poke. Consumer preferences are unpredictable. They shift on a whim, blah, blah, blah. I already know all this. I've heard it from colleagues, friends, family, even my business partner. They all warned me over and over about the uncertainties, about how literally every single thing could go wrong.

That didn't stop me from wanting it. My open-flame restaurant. I'd made it real in my heart, and I just had to see it with my own two eyes. I had to know if I could make it as magical and wonderful as I'd imagined it. I didn't care about the odds of failing. I had to try.

Once the crisscrossed log structure is about chest height, we use it as a frame to support more logs, and it starts to look like a tee-pee fence, and oh yes, it's as big and impressive as I was hoping. My grandma would have never let us build it this tall.

"Opening a restaurant is a huge gamble, incredibly risky." Another jab, and again I wince, but I also grit my teeth against a snarl.

"I am aware," I say, biting back the litany of curse words I feel like hurling at him. All I wanted from this evening was a giant bonfire and to relive the lovely Christmas Eve tradition from my childhood. Instead, I'm getting skewered in the chest by the guest I didn't invite. Anger and irritation tense along my spine. He needs to shut up about this.

"Costs fluctuate. You never know what you're going to be spending. And your marketing, fuck, that has to be pitch perfect. Operations, cash flow, staffing, there's so much to manage. And even if, by some miracle, you do get all that right, you still have to be incredibly lucky."

Right. That's it.

I stomp over to him and, with all my weight and both hands flat on his chest, I shove him. "Shut up! It failed, okay? It burned up on the launchpad. Is that what you want to hear?" My voice is loud, but there's a warble to it, and my eyes sting.

My shove doesn't pack the punch I'd hoped for. I wanted to lay him out on his ass, but a faulty half step is all I get from him. A little stumble. Highly unsatisfying, and I'm considering pushing him again when he raises his hand in a pose of innocent-defense. "I'm just trying to make you feel better," he says, clearly baffled by my response.

"*What?* How is that supposed to make me feel better?"

"Because you're better off."

I stare at him, bewildered. "In what world am I better off?" I'm broke with no restaurant, no job, and my current housing status is *not* not-homeless.

He grimaces and he huffs and turns away as if to stomp off. But he thinks better of it and turns back. "Let's just say I speak from experience."

"What experience?" I blink at him, confused.

"No," he shakes his head. "A demon's life is very private. You shouldn't ask. It's incredibly rude, especially if you ask about a business venture. Just, no. We're not *'sharers'* like you humans." He throws up air quotes around the word 'sharers.' "Just take my word for it. I know what —"

He cuts himself off and shifts uncomfortably from foot to foot. I can feel the tug of a bemused smile at the corner of my lips. I bite it back. His mouth opens with an inhale like he's ready to say something, but then it snaps shut, opens, snaps shut, and I nearly laugh. I can't put a finger on exactly why but, despite my raised hackles, I still manage to find his flustered discomfort amusing. He wants to tell me something, but he's fighting with himself, and it's so, well, cute.

"Stop looking at me like that." He straightens up, brow furrowing.

"Like what?" I ask, and my smile grows even bigger. It makes him even more uncomfortable, and I cannot describe just how adorable it is to watch a big, black-eyed demon swing from offended to conflicted and back to offended, all with very little provocation.

"Like that. I don't even know what to call it," he points at my face, wiggling a finger at me. "But stop it."

"Was it a restaurant?" I ask. "You opened a restaurant, and it failed." It's the obvious guess, but a good place to start.

He glares at me, but even with those black eyes and those great big horns, he doesn't scare me. "It's personal," he growls, and this time, he flashes his sharp teeth at me. I pull up, squaring my shoulders and crossing my arms. I can't believe his hypocrisy.

"It *is* personal, isn't it? Incredibly personal. Now imagine how violating it would be for someone to stick their giant, red hands right into a box full of your business documents, read them, and then start peppering you with intrusive questions!" I'm back to being irritated, but I'm also a little smug because I'm clearly making an excellent point and that always feels good.

"You *gave* me the box," he says.

"Not to snoop through!"

"You didn't say that. I said I'd start the fire; you gave me the box. It was a fair exchange. If there were stipulations, you should have laid them out ahead of time."

"Not everything is a bargain!" I throw my hands up in the air.

He rolls his eyes. "So say humans."

"Okay, let's say it was a bargain. I gave you access to my papers, but I called it a *burn box*, which clearly defined its purpose and established my permissions for use: you were allowed to burn anything within. But you *read* from the box, overstepping and violating our agreement. Which means now you owe me." My smugness blooms, puffing my chest.

His eyes narrow, but his mouth twists into an incredulous half-smile that shows off the points of his teeth on one side. "Devilry," he mutters and shakes his head, but there's a touch of something in his voice that waters my blooming smugness.

"One question," he says. It's clearly an opening offer.

"Five," I counter.

"Two."

"Three," I cross my arms.

"Two."

"*Three.*"

"Agreed." He extends his arm to me, and I reach for his hand, meaning to shake it. He pulls back. "No. Like this." He grabs my forearm, and I mimic him, wrapping my fingers as far around his muscled forearm as they'll reach. "If you're going to bargain like a demon, you might as well shake like one." My breath hitches unexpectedly at the minimal contact, and my fingers stroke his arm all on their own.

"Very nice texture," I say, clearing my throat. Obviously, I was feeling the cashmere. He is zero percent fooled. I can tell by the smoldering-orange flicker I catch in his eye. I recognize it from last night.

We shake once and release.

"Ask," he says, but the way he tightens up, I can tell his answers are only going to be as good as my questions.

"Let me think," I say. I start stuffing the wood-frame bonfire structure with small kindling and tinder bundles made of dried leaves and the last of the paper from the burn box. I want the structure to burn evenly, so I've got to stuff it uniformly throughout. He joins me, helping with the work without my having to ask or bargain.

"Okay, here's my first question," I say. "What were the significant moments in the life of your business that either gave you confidence it would succeed or made you worry that it would fail?"

He freezes, mouth popping open and giving me a look that is somewhere between offended and surprised. "That is *not* one question."

I blink at him innocently. "Just because it's an excellent question, doesn't mean it's not a single question. Answer it."

"Now who's overstepping?" He grumbles. He's quiet for a long time, but I can tell he's getting his thoughts together, so I let him be.

"It was a decade ago. And it was a bar, not a restaurant, though we added a small menu at one point," he says. "When I turned twenty-one, my father gifted me an 'investment egg'. It's a tradition in my family." He's starting at the very beginning, I note. I like that. "Having that much cash was the first thing that unduly inflated my confidence. With all that money, how could I fail?"□

He describes in detail the classy, high-end club with roof-top access and downtown views that he and a friend opened together. By his account, it was very swanky with a cocktail program that I can't help but be impressed by. Adventurous flavors, experimental textures. I would have loved to have tried them.□

"We managed to keep it open for three years. It bled cash the whole time, and when it folded—" He shakes his head. "It was humiliating. My older brothers all listened to my father. They looked for quick flips and doubled their money on their first investments, but I opted for a passion project, like some bright-eyed, rosy-cheeked, imbecilic cherub. It was a horrifying disgrace. It embarrassed my whole family, but especially my father."

I only nod. I have a feeling if I interrupt him, he'll clam up, and I want all the details. I'm equally curious and envious. Three years? I would have killed for that long.

As he continues, he lays out the significant moments, the ups and downs, just like I asked for, but he peppers in warnings, determined to turn it into a cautionary tale. "It's a lot like gambling. You lay your money down knowing the odds are stacked against you, but with a passion project, it's a whole lot harder to walk away from the table. Even as you watch your stack of chips dwindle, you keep telling yourself it's okay. If you just stick it out, in the end you won't lose. But you do. Everyone does. That's why only fools gamble."

I'm quiet for a moment as I take that in. "I thought demons loved gambling." The thought jumps from my head straight out of my mouth. I'm not sure if it's rude to say, but they own all the biggest casinos in the country, including the one at the Emberlight Resort. It's not unfounded.

"That's question two," he says.

"No, it's not!" I protest.

"It is. And the answer is: not this demon. As a kid maybe, but not anymore." He continues with his story, and I love all the details, the worry, the work, the hard decisions. It's a story with an unhappy ending, but even so, I can't help but smile at the vicarious thrill of someone's dream coming to life.

He sees my smile. "It was a bad investment," he says sternly.

"I know." It's true even if I don't like hearing it.

"A gamble!"

"I know!"

"Then why do you look so, so... inspired?"

"I'm not! I'm the opposite of inspired. I'm—purging." I gesture to the bonfire, pointing out the tinder bundles made of crumpled paper. "My menu ideas, floor plan, logo and website mockups, the start of a training manual, the last pages of the lease agreement, and every scrap of an idea that I ever jotted down. I'm letting it all go tonight. Satisfied?"

"Question three," he says, pointing at me.

I roll my eyes. I got a lot of mileage out of my first question, so I don't argue.

He looks at me, hard and assessing until he arrives at his verdict. "I'm satisfied. What are your plans now?" He asks.

"A question for a question?" We've come to the end of our bargain. So, I offer him new terms.

His eyes narrow at me again, a look I'm getting a lot this evening, but he agrees. "Fine."

"You're looking at it," I say as I strike a match. I have no plans beyond this—hiding away for the holidays and letting a certain canceled opening date pass me by. New Year's Eve. We were going to open with a bang, a huge party during the Truthfire Festival. Instead, I'll spend New Year's here with a case of wine and a five-pound block of cheese. After the first of the year, I'll figure something out, but until then, just this.

I light the tinder bundles and they catch. I know it doesn't make sense to most people, but fire is how I discovered myself. I feel a bond I can't explain. Others say they feel guardian angels or the spirits of their ancestors guiding their steps. For me, it's fire.

The pieces of kindling catch next, and maybe ten minutes later, the logs start to burn. Samite and I stand in the warm glow and comfortable silence broken only by the crackling and whispering of the fire, and I'm glad he's here. It feels right. A bonfire is meant to be shared.

The sun sets, turning the sky overhead a deep purple, but the larger the flames grow, the brighter and lighter I feel. The crushing weight of disappointment that I've carried around for the last few months lifts off my chest, and I'm filled with a boundless sense of freedom.

I spread my arms wide, basking in the waves of heat rolling off the roaring fire, and out of the corner of my eye, I see Samite doing the same.

Chapter 6
Samite

Fire is a magnet that stirs the deep recesses of the mind. Transfixed by the bonfire's dancing flame, the world fades, and I'm beckoned inward to the meditative void, a place my mother used to call the soul's abyss.

When I was young, she would make my four brothers and me name ten gods from the pantheon every night before bed. On new moons, she'd dress us in hooded robes and drag us into the woods for nights of ritual worship. Back then, she hoped one of us would feel the Dark Mother's calling and take the mark of the devout, but she was disappointed by all of us.

As her youngest, I had the privilege of watching her last spark of hope dim and die with me. Five sons and we all took after our father, worshiping at the altar of capitalism and turning our backs on the mysteries and mysticism of our mother's deeply held religion.

I never told her, but there were nights when I felt I don't know what. Something. Not the burning, and I never heard Mother Darkness's voice. But on nights like tonight, I connected with the fire. I traveled inward and found something primal and alive. It danced in me back then the same way it dances in me tonight, the tongues of flame syncing with the beat of my heart.

I am alive.

The logs settle with a crash and a burst of sparks, and I return from the void. Blinking, I look around. Sofia is no longer standing at my side, and an uncomfortable pang shoots through my chest. My hand automatically rises to rub the spot.

She's gone. Loneliness echoes through me.

"Welcome back." I turn to the sound of her voice. "You were gone a long time," she says. She's hunkered down under a blanket, shivering, but there's a blissed-out smile half-hidden behind a steaming mug. My insides leap at the sight of her.

Sofia has made a seat out of a log, and I join her on it, dropping down so close, our knees and elbows bump, and the little touches chase away the lonely echo.

She smiles up at me, her face glowing, and my head swims. I smile back. Her radiance and the flickers of happiness in her eyes are as warm and transfixing as the fire.

This is not good. I'm supposed to be executing my new game plan tonight, but honestly, I don't have one. I've come up short. Offering her money didn't work. Seduction didn't work. I'm not about to threaten her. That's low and unseemly. What's more, I can't seem to summon the will to think up a new scheme right now.

If there really isn't a way off this mountain, then I'm stuck here until the roads open. Humans lie at the drop of a hat, but if they have to carry the lie for longer than, say, a single conversation, they tend to crumble, and Sofia hasn't slipped even once. So, there it is. I'm stuck here. I wait for the panic and fury to set in, but they don't. I glance at the bonfire, then back at Sofia. Where is my impetus to be gone from this place? I am mired by a soul-deep contentment I couldn't have anticipated finding tonight.

"Where do you go when you get caught up in the fire?" she asks, nudging me with her shoulder.

I catch a whiff of something herbal and savory steaming from her mug, and my stomach grumbles. "Somewhere without food," I say, easily dodging another of her personal questions, and she laughs.

"We have *caldo de pollo*, chicken soup, in this one, and *champurrado*, the best kind of hot chocolate, in this one." She holds up two thermoses, but that's not all there is. She's turned the empty sled into a table, and on it sits an assortment of treats in red tins. She names them for me, "All the holiday favorites: *buñuelos, pan de polvo, y caramelos.*"

When did she have time to make all this? It took me three hours just to wash the clothes I'm wearing right now.

She pours me a mug of soup. I take a long inhale of the delectable steam before I sip. It tastes of rich stock and herbs. Divine. The woman has a gift.

Time slipped away while I was in the void, and the night sky has gone inky black. Our seven-foot bonfire has burnt down to a third of its size. It still casts light and warmth, but the flaming tower is long gone. We consumed it.

"I haven't done something like this in a long time," I say, breaking the comfortable silence, but if I were being completely honest, I'd have to say I've never done anything quite like this. Sipping soup by a fire all cute and cozy? Never.

"Yeah," she says with a wistful sigh. "It's been a while for me too. When I was a kid, we did this all the time. It was our Christmas Eve tradition. Back then, most of my family worked at the Emberlight Resort, still do actually, so they've never had holidays off. It's the busy season. My grandma would bring all the grandkids up to the cabin, twelve of us with sleeping bags," she chuckles. "And we'd have a bonfire every Christmas Eve. I always thought there was a special meaning behind it. It felt like an old tradition, but one day I asked her, and she said it was just a way to tire us out. We'd gather and chop wood for hours, so excited for the big bonfire, but it was just a trick." She laughs, but I catch a note of disappointment.

"What about your family?" she asks. "Aren't they missing you for the holidays?"

More personal questions. Humans are notoriously blind to their own intrusiveness. It's just who they are. They bump into a complete stranger and exchange fifty personal details like it's nothing. And online, holy depths of hell, they shovel their personal information out there like they can't post it fast enough. But demons know better. We never give anything away for free.￼

"Are we still doing a question for a question?" I ask. I should negotiate for better terms, but I'm feeling generous and soft because of her glowing face and the general sense of fondness burnt into me by the fire. Plus, she did make this delicious soup. And cookies. I pick up a small cookie, *pan de polvo*, and pop it into my mouth. "Fuck me, they're good," I mumble. Sweet and spicy with a crumble that somehow melts in a very satisfying way.

"Sure, a question for a question," she says with a lopsided grin. Her big, dark eyes are blinking slower than usual, like they would if she were very relaxed or inebriated. *Firebliss* is a thing, but only for demons as far as I know, yet Sofia has the shine of it all over her. It's beautiful.

"No one is missing me yet," I say, answering her question.

Nobody loves Christmas more than demons. It's a season marked by a frenzy of unchecked spending, an orgy of commercial desire, and a symphony of cash registers ringing in the season. But when it comes to observing the holiday and its odd assortment of traditions, we don't.

"But if I'm not home on True Ember's Day, that's New Year's Eve for you, I'll definitely hear about it."

"From your wife?" she asks, her words a little mumbled.

I turn to give her a look, but she's staring intently into her mug of soup, and so I study her profile. If she were fae, she'd have the dainty, smooth features everyone raves about. But Sofia has pronounced features, prominent cheekbones and a full mouth. The angles of her face catch light and cast shadows. There are depths to behold, and for a moment, I'm lost in them.

"That counts as another question," I say, snapping out of it. "I don't have a wife. My mother is devout, a strict observer of the Silent Hour, and she expects me home every year." I feel another unexpected flash of fondness as I picture my mother's table set for the traditional feast held at full dark on True Ember's Day. What is wrong with me tonight?

Two days ago, I'd all but decided to skip holidays with the family to stay in town for the Festival. The Truthfire Festival is to Winter Bliss, Idaho, what Mardi Gras is to New Orleans, Louisiana, only more seismically spectacular. It's a melding of the secular New Year and the religious True Embers Day celebrations. The Festival organizers orchestrate a volcanic eruption every year at the stroke of midnight. It's said to be an epic show of demon magic. Before I landed on this mountain, I'd been thinking that I might stick around for the spectacle. Tonight, I don't know how I feel. Different. Nostalgic. And a little raw, but there's nothing pulling at me. I'm good just being here.

I glance at Sofia again, and I'm struck by a poetic thought—she has the beauty of a natural wonder, a brooding storm, or a windswept canyon. Even a violently erupting volcano would pale in comparison to her.

"Are you cold?" she asks. I hadn't really noticed, but now that she's mentioned it.

"I'm a bit chilly," I say.

"I'm happy to share." She lifts her arm, extending her blanket towards me and revealing her awful wardrobe of layered plaid that, by some trick of the firelight, looks more inviting than awful right now.

I scoot close and pull the corner of her blanket to wrap my shoulders. Warmth moves between us. Not heat. Warmth. There's a glow in my chest that grows brighter as she presses in at my side. My arm circles her and there's a pulse of warmth everywhere we touch. Her head comes to rest on my chest, and the glow that was already too bright threatens to blind me. I should be concerned, but instead, I'm overwhelmed by a desire to squeeze her. So, I do. With both arms, I pull her in as tight and as close as I can, tucking her against me. It feels amazing.

She gives a contented little sigh. "You're very warm," she murmurs against my chest, and considering I had my tongue inside her last night, this shouldn't feel particularly intimate, but it does. My body sinks into the moment the way teeth sink into a marshmallow, with ease and giddy delight. It's mildly alarming, but even as I try to take stock of the profound coziness, my cheek comes to rest on top of her head. We're practically strangers, but tonight we're as comfortable as old friends. How did this happen?

Her shiny black hair catches the flickering orange glow of the fire. She smells of smoke and faintly of citrus and berry. I close my eyes and take a deep breath. Her scent fills my nose then travels deeper, imprinting on me, and I know that if I tilt her chin up and kiss her, her taste will imprint on me too. It's a bad idea, but I want to do it anyway.

"Who pushed you out of the helicopter?" she asks, and the hand I was about to lift stays put at my side.

"Hush. It's not your turn." I say, and she snorts a little laugh, but now I'm stalling. I need a minute to let go of the need to kiss her. This night is masked in mildness, but there's a thread of intensity just below the surface, and I keep plucking it. It's just the fire, I tell myself again, but I'm not reassured. I've been to countless bonfires in my lifetime, but I've never done this. I've fought, drank, prayed, sang, danced, screamed, and fucked by a fire, but I've never cuddled with someone. It's strangely potent.□

She nudges me with her knee. "Hurry up and ask your question so that I can ask mine."

"Right," I say with a little shake of my head. Talking is a good distraction. "Who's Ryan?" I ask. It's a question I've wanted an answer to all day.

She stiffens. "Ask something else."

"No. You got to hear all about my failed venture. It's your turn. Spill."

She's quiet for a while, and when she does speak, she's cryptic, but Ryan's a fiendish asshole. That's about the sum of it. I figured as much, but it's worse than I'd imagined. I'd assumed he'd talked her into entering the venture with too little funding, a tale as old as time, but no, Ryan had the money; he just didn't see it through.

"He backed out on a deal?" My teeth grind over the words, and my temper flares, burning holes in the hazy cloud of coziness. I want to hurt him. "Give me his address, and I'll pay him a visit."

"What would that change?" she says, and there's not even a sliver of steel in her voice.

"The shape of his skull," I say, and it's a promise. A bargain is sacred, and if I break some of his bones, Ryan will remember that next time. "He really didn't give you any reason for backing out?" I ask, bewildered.

She's quiet.

I rephrase my question. "He just left town and didn't say anything?" It's hard to comprehend. "Are you sure he wasn't murdered?" That seems more likely. "Have you checked the morgue?"

"It's my turn to ask a question," she says. "I want to know about the helicopter and how you got yourself dumped onto my lake."

"Would you like the full story with all the details?" I ask.

"I would," she says with a firm nod. I take a finger and lift her chin until our eyes meet, and again, I'm fighting a desperate urge to kiss her. Instead, I give her a look, and it takes her a second, but she catches my meaning.

"Fine," she rolls her eyes. "We got drunk one night celebrating some very good news, and one thing led to another. We started to fool around." As she speaks, the color in her face rises, but not in a lusty, fun way. She's embarrassed. "Up to that point, our relationship had been strictly professional, and we should have kept it that way. When our clothes started coming off, he—" She clears her throat. "He stopped things and left. The next thing I knew, he was backing out on our partnership."

"He's married," I say. It's so obvious.

"No."

"*No?* Did you laugh at the size of his dick?"

"No! We didn't get that far."

"You had to have done something." I insist.

She grits her teeth and refuses to answer until I nudge her and then with a salty side-eye she says, "He didn't find me attractive, ok?"

"Bullshit. You're as fuckable as they come." It's not flattery. It's the truth.

"You haven't seen me completely naked."

"Is that an invitation?" My arm circles further around her, tugging at her waist. "Because if it is, I accept." There's a note of teasing in my voice but, "I'm dead serious. I'd love to see you naked." Half-naked wasn't enough, but that's so much worse than a kiss. What am I doing?

She looks up at me. Her eyes are narrowed, but she's trying to hide a smile. Her mouth twists to one side, and it's not working. She's doing a terrible job.

"Now it's definitely your turn to answer. Tell me about the helicopter. Feel free to omit a detail or two, just to keep things fair," she says.

I'm not actually sure I do owe her an answer. I've lost track. It's very unlike me, but nevertheless, here we go. I take a deep breath, and for a split second, I consider lying. She'd never know. I'm not above lying to keep the details of my life private, but a question for a question is as straightforward a deal as they come. And unlike Ryan, I don't back out on deals. That's not to say that they always go as planned...

"I had a deal lined up, a solid new venture, very promising," I begin. I tell her briefly about my months of market-gap research, the vetting steps I took to evaluate my potential partners, and all the other various due diligences I checked off prior to arriving in Winter Bliss. There's something satisfying about laying this part out, like I'm stating my case before a jury, proving beyond any shadow of a doubt that I did everything right in the lead up. I was calculating and shrewd. Nobody can say I wasn't.

She nods, not interrupting, and as I talk, something strange happens. A weight lifts, and I'm soothed by the outpouring of private details I should be carefully guarding. There's no anxiousness, no worry about exposure. Bizarre. I keep going, adding details I'm not strictly obligated to share per our agreement, but my instincts are being overridden by a new urge to—*vent*. Holy Mother Darkness, forgive me. It's such a despicably human thing to do.

"I didn't trust some of the other people at the table. So, before coming, I convinced my would-be partner to take me on as the sole investor. It meant assuming more of the risk, and I had to front a lot more cash than I'd planned to, but I'd done my homework. The potential for a substantial payday was there. It was justified."

She continues to nod. The jury is clearly on my side, but I pause because I'm embarrassed to share what comes next. She must sense it. Her hand slides over mine, the one I've tucked in at her waist. She laces our fingers together, a small gesture, but I like her hand wrapped around mine immensely. Not good. I've seen scenes like this play out before; a human reaches out to touch another human's hand or shoulder, and what follows is a horror show. A dam breaks. The person cries while verbally vomiting all over them both. Disgusting. I will never do that. I refuse.

I meet her eye as suspicion forms. She blinks back at me innocently, but I'm not sure I buy it. I've always assumed humans have no magic, but what if they have a diabolical form of magic that pulls secrets from the soul? It's a terrifying thought. But also—what a devilishly good trick. Fuck. My estimation of humans keeps rising the longer I'm around Sofia. I'll have to acquaint myself with lesser humans when I leave this place so that I can go back to thinking of them as unsophisticated and unremarkable beings. I prefer that.

"When a new partnership is formed between demons, initial investments are almost always delivered in cash. It's symbolic and a sign of respect," I tell her, and I explain that what's deeply disrespectful is showing up with the wrong amount of cash. "The officiant accountant said I was short. I still don't know how it happened, but it doesn't matter. It was an unforgivable offense. My partner was rightly outraged. He tore up our contract and set the table on fire."

"And then he threw you out of a helicopter?"

"No, that wasn't him. He's probably gone back and reopened negotiations with some of the other potential investors." I can't keep the pang of frustration and hurt out of my voice. I should have followed him and groveled. Instead, I went to the bar and then the casino.

"I don't know who the idiots with the helicopter were, but I know what they were after. I left the cash for my deal in my hotel room, and I may have drunkenly mentioned it to someone that night. A stupid slip-up. Not surprisingly, I was jumped as soon as I stumbled out of the casino." She gives a gratifying little gasp. The jury is eating out of my hand.

"They wanted my money, but I refused to give it to them. I assume they thought dangling me out of a helicopter would change my mind. I'd guess they didn't mean to drop me until I'd told them the code to my room, but I'm heavier than I look. And as I said before, they were idiots."

"At least you're fine. Not even a sprained ankle. And your money is safe, right? They didn't get it."

I shrug. "I doubt they gave up after the helicopter. They probably headed right back to the hotel to see if they could find a way into my room."

"But you locked it up, didn't you?" she asks. She reminds me that there are safes in every hotel room at the resort, and very cutely, she says she thinks they're good ones, like I don't know a Mammon Strongbox when I see one. They're not just good. They're top of the line with cutting-edge technology. Theft-proof and impregnable. There is no safer place to keep cash or valuables than inside a Mammon Strongbox.

"I left the money on the bed in a leather travel bag, partially unzipped. If the helicopter hooligans made it into my room, they have it. If not, a snooping maid could have walked off with it by now." I was a dozen drinks deep by the time I dropped the bag off and headed to the casino. I was angry, embarrassed, drunk, not thinking. It's no excuse.

"No!" Her hands fly to her mouth, and she stares at me with a mix of incredulity and pity. I flush all over with shame, and my stomach turns. I've been an idiot many times over. I'm not sure what I'll find when I get back to the resort on Mount BZB, but as uncomfortable as the worry and shame is, it's not consuming me tonight.

There's not much else to say. I can't think of anything, and neither can she. No more questions to exchange. So, we sit in silence. She cuddles up tighter at my side and offers me more soup, but I'm not hungry.

"*Champurrado?* I slipped some rum in it." She shakes the thermos and winks at me.

"No, thank you." She wraps my hand in both of hers and snuggles her head against my shoulder.

At midnight, she jumps up and says it's time to put out the fire. There's not much of it left, only one intact log, and I think we should let it burn out. She grabs a pail and starts heaping snow onto the dying flames. It's an ignoble death for such a magnificent bonfire, and I refuse to help.

"Just let it die naturally," I say.

"No. It's time," she insists.

We walk back to her cabin in silence except for the jingling of silver bells, and I find my eyes drawn skyward. It's been a strange night, and I can't seem to shake the feeling that the stars are unnaturally close, pressing in. But when I look up, they recede back into the heavens, as impossibly far away as always.

"Sofia," I say her name, and she turns to look at me with an expectant half smile. "Nothing, never mind." I just wanted her to look at me, and when she does, I feel better, like I'm staring into a fire again.

Chapter 7
Sofia

Samite walks a half-step behind me, pulling *La Roja* without my having to ask. He's been quiet a long time, and I can't help wondering what he's thinking about. I hope it's something pleasant, but I know he has plenty to worry about.

What an idiot I've been. A demon gets pushed from a helicopter, and I assume that being stranded is his only problem. When he came to after being abducted, threatened, dropped on his head, knocked out cold, and left for dead, he was rude to me, and I was quick to take offense. But if our roles had been reversed, I would have behaved so much worse.

"Sofia." He speaks, and I light up at the sound of his voice. Sofia is a good name, I've never disliked it, but it's so much better when Samite says it. He strums it with his tongue, and I feel it between my legs. Every time. I look at him, attention fixed.

"Nothing. Never mind."

For a brief moment, I'm disappointed, but then he blinks at me. His eyelashes fall closed in a slow sweep, and when they open again, our eyes lock. A warm spark ignites inside me, and I smile. He smiles back. A cozy silence settles between us, and we continue walking.

⁂

By the time we get to the cabin, it's half past midnight, officially Christmas Day. The warmth of the bonfire is long gone, and the night's deep chill has burrowed its way through my layers. Inside, the tree lights are on. The colored bulbs cast a twinkling glow but no warmth, and I shiver. As if on cue, the rickety heater kicks on with a metal groan.

Samite crosses the living room and flops down on the couch. He slumps over, going sideways as if settling in for the night. The least I can do is show him how the bed folds out, I think to myself, but when I come to a stop in front of him, what I say is, "I have a queen bed. It's roomy and a lot more comfortable than this couch."

He tilts his head up to look at me. "Are you bragging or inviting me to your bed?" he asks, and his gold studs twinkle at me from above the shadow of his heavy brow.

"Inviting. I thought you could use a good night's sleep." It's a lie. There was no thought. Words just fell from my mouth.

"I won't stay on my side." He crosses his arms. "Or keep my hands to myself." What an adorably honest demon. I press my lips to hold back a smile even as the thought of him in my bed makes me flush warm.

"I don't mind roaming hands if you don't," I say, crossing my arms, mirroring him. What is this, I wonder, a stand-off? A bargain? Either way, I like it.

He rises to his feet, terms accepted, and as I lead the way, he follows, stripping his clothes. I gawk unabashedly over my shoulder and knock right into the wall. *Thud.* I correct course, and by the time we're inside my bedroom, he's fully naked, and he's a sight to behold. The beats of my heart falter as my eyes roam up his deep red skin to the tip of his curved horns. If there's still a chill in the cabin, I can't feel it now.

As he rounds to the far side of the bed, he pauses to fold his clothes and place them neatly on a chair, and I don't know why I find that so endearing, but my heart glows at the sight of it. A goofy grin spreads across my face. I fight to hide it.

"What?" he says, turning too soon.

I smother the grin behind a polite offer of a shirt, shorts, something to sleep in.

"No." He shakes his head, firmly. "I'd prefer you sleep naked as well."

I swallow hard and start stripping. When I'm down to my white t-shirt and panties, I stop.

"Is this how you're comfortable?" he asks.

"I don't know," I answer honestly. My head is too fuzzy to think.

He throws back the comforter and climbs into bed. From there, he watches me. I wouldn't say it makes me self-conscious, just very aware of my body. Of how my knee sinks into the bed, how my hips shift as I climb in, how my breasts rise and fall as I come to rest on my side, facing him.

There's maybe a foot between us, not much space at all, and this close, it's so easy to see the orange embers when they flicker to life at the back of his coal-black eyes. For a moment, it's like I'm back at the bonfire, and there's a promise of losing myself if I stare for too long.

My hands itch to touch him. I have explicit permission to let my hands roam, and even if I didn't, there's an invitation written all over his face. I want to run my fingers through his hair, caress along his jaw, and feel his lips against the pad of my thumb. I want to know all the intimate textures of him. But then he'll learn mine. He'll see the rough patches and feel the places that should be smooth but aren't.

I turn over and hit the switch on the bedside lamp, plunging the room into darkness. I whisper a soft "good night" over my shoulder.

"Good night, Sofia." He strums my name and reaches for me. His arm circles my waist, just above my hips, and he pulls my backside into the spoon of his body, a perfect fit. I melt against him, sighing in delight as his warmth wraps me in a safe and snug little bubble.

Bliss.

We spoon for a while, and I'm content until he shifts against me. It's a good feeling, and I can't help a soft groan. He shifts again, and I press into him. His hands begin to roam, setting off a nervous flutter in my chest, but his hand moves down, away from my waist to slide over the curve of my hip, trailing tingles all over the unscarred, smooth skin. I let out another soft groan.

His breath quickens behind my ear, and as his hand moves from my thigh to my hip, it slides under my panties, then roams back to squeeze my ass.

"So fuckable," he mutters, and his cock nudges my backside, right between the clefts of my cheeks. Heat pools between my legs and my head spins.

"Mmmm. You really like this." His hips rock lightly against me.

He's not wrong, but an unnerving thought pops into my head. "Can—can you smell me?"

"Like a dog? No." He chuckles dismissively. "Our tongues are sensitive. I guess you could say I taste you, but it's the chemistry of excitement and fear that I taste, not what's happening between your legs. Although, in this case, I'm guessing they are one and the same." It's a fascinating ability, but an unfair advantage. I'm not sure I like it. His hand roams again, this time dipping between my legs, and I'm distracted. He doesn't linger any longer than it takes to verify that he's right before his hand moves to my belly, another smooth place. No worries there.

"This is where you're the most biteable. When you were laid out on the butcher block, I wanted to sink my teeth in right here." His hand kneads just below my belly button, and under his palm, my softness feels sexy, especially when he rumbles wordlessly into my ear, prickling my skin with awareness.

"And these, Sofia. These." His hand slides under my shirt to palm my breasts, first one then the other. The skin is mostly smooth, all but a tiny patch on my left breast. I doubt he'll notice, especially if his head is swimming like mine. He continues working my breasts, his hardened cock pressing against my ass.

He groans, and I feel the points of his teeth make light contact with my shoulder. I shiver in a very delicious way. "I want to lick. And suck." He plucks at one nipple and then the other, and they respond to his touch, pebbling and eager for more. "And then I want to slide my cock right here."

He runs his fingers down my sternum, between my breasts, "and fuck your tits."

I flush hot, head to toe. And a needy throb pulses between my legs. It sends me out of my right mind. I sit up and strip off my shirt before I can change my mind. "Do it," I say as I fall back to the bed. I want him to. I grab my breasts, squeezing them together. As soon as he said it, the idea of him fucking my tits derailed my brain, and now I need it.

In the darkness, I feel Samite rise from the bed. The mattress groans as he climbs over me, his knees caging my ribs. Excitement pulses in my veins for a heartbeat before reality catches up to me. It's pitch black in the room, but the moment he touches me, he'll feel it, the textured skin along my side.

He freezes. "You're afraid," he says.

"It's nothing," I say automatically. Maybe he'll be distracted enough not to feel it. I reach for his cock to help guide him to my chest, but he bats my hand away. "No." He stretches in the direction of the side table.

"Not the lamp!"

He returns to resting on his heels, but he snaps his fingers and a small flame leaps to life in his palm. I yelp in surprise. The flame flickers like a candle, comforting even as I try to sink into the bed and hide.

Samite's eyes roam slowly over me as he takes in my entire torso, every flawed inch of it: the skin graft scars on my left shoulder and side, the rippling burn marks that stretch out in every direction down my arm, across my ribs, and a little way up the side of my breast.

He's quiet for too long, and I start to squirm.

He reaches for my left breast with the hand not holding the flame, and he cups it as his thumb glides gently back and forth over my nipple. I suck in a breath.

"Did you know that ancient demons believed that the reason fire burns is because it contains twin spirits?" I shake my head, just a quick little jerk, and he continues. "It's the only twin element in nature, the only one in constant conflict with itself. Friction begets fire." His thumb keeps moving, slow and steady, as his black eyes with their orange glow stare into me. "It can never decide if it wants to be safety or danger, benevolent or cruel, and so it's often both at once." He plucks at my nipple and my breath hitches again. "May I?" he asks, as his hand moves to hover over my shoulder, the worst of my scarring.

I hesitate a second before I nod. My heart races as his palm touches down on my patchwork of skin. "To love the twin-spirited flame is both a blessing and a curse, and those born with fire in their nature will always love it, no matter the price." His voice is low and full of reverence.

His tongue flicks the air. "This is what you're afraid of?"

With my heart still racing, I nod. It's not that I want to lie, but I feel a twinge of irritation when I realize that if I did lie, I wouldn't get away with it, thanks to his tongue.

"The scars or the fire that caused them?"

"The scars," I answer. It wasn't the fire's fault. It was mine. I was naïve, careless, and irresponsible. I'll bear the reminder for the rest of my life.

"You are beautiful, Sofia. Maria. Moreno." His tongue strums over each of my names slowly, pausing between them. I feel the rolling sounds down deep, and I wish I had a hundred names because with each one he says in that voice of his, something tentative and coiled inside me relaxes. "Intensely and unquestionably dazzling," he murmurs.

His eyes are hypnotic, and I'm already falling into the orange glow before I'm beckoned further by the tendrils of smoke that start wisping up from the outer corners.

I let out a small gasp as hot desire floods my body.

There's a shift in the direction my blood is pumping, and he must taste the change because when his tongue flicks again, he smiles a wolfish smile that shows off the points of his teeth.

The little fire in his palm goes out and, cloaked in darkness, he whispers to me, "I want to see you." There's a pang in his voice, a longing that I understand because I feel it too. The moment the light went out, I missed the sight of him, his smoking eyes, his smile, his horns, his face, his everything.

I reach out and turn on the lamp.

He sighs but there's a guttural moan beneath it, and the smoke is livelier now, streaming from his eyes and circling above his head in a dark halo. He's beautiful beyond words.

I want him. I want to devour him and for him to devour me. I grab his forearms, meaning to pull his mouth to mine, but the moment I touch him, I hear it.

Always know exactly how and when you'll stop a burn before you start it.

I'm stunned, and I go still.

"What now?" he asks, stiffening again.

I've never heard those words when touching a person. Samite is the first. I don't understand. He isn't a flame I need to tend to or a fire that could burn me—or is he?

His eyes smoke and smolder.

He draws me.

If I lose myself in him, what kind of scar will he leave when he goes?

"They'll clear the road in a few more days," I say. I don't know exactly when, but they've never taken more than a week. "That's when this burn ends."

"Burn?" He gives me a puzzled look.

"Fire safety," I answer vaguely. It doesn't make sense to him, but it's vitally important to me. Samite may be a wholly new kind of fire, but I'm not the naïve and irresponsible girl I was the first time I got burned. A planned end and a little caution is called for. This fire we're starting can't last. The moment he's free to leave, burn over.

He doesn't press for an explanation, only makes a noise of acknowledgement, and then runs his hands over my skin. "You've cooled. Would you like me to warm you up?" His grin is back, and all I have to do is bite my lip, and he has his answer.

I expect him to scoot straight down, but instead he stretches out longways across the bed until our bodies are in the shape of a 'T', his head at my hip. He pulls my panties down past my knees, and I kick them the rest of the way off. He settles on his side, and lifts my nearest leg over his head, spreading me wide, and draping it over his rib cage. I'm open and exposed, and he's not shy about taking in the view. He makes an appreciative noise, then lowers his head. His mouth greets me with a few flicks of his tongue.

That's all it takes to warm me back up. Heat blooms inside. He nudges my outer leg to make more room for his head, and even then, the bend of his horns presses into the flesh of my thigh, adding to the thrill already thrumming through my body.

His tongue sinks into me and I gasp. His thumb finds the perfect spot and rubs a slow circle, and I'm panting. He sets a rhythm. His tongue thrusts in and out at the same speed his thumb circles. My hips roll on their own.

In and out, round and round, and both of my hands fist the covers beneath me, pressure and pleasure building.

He hums and nuzzles into me. Then continues with the in and out, and I cry out at the first little spasm. He picks up the pace with his thumb, his tongue keeps up the steady thrusts, and I come with a moan. He moans back as more spasms shake me, clenching out waves of pleasure that travel all the way to my toes. "*¡Qué bárbaro!*" I call out with breathless wonder, and he chuckles.

As my vision clears, I'm treated to the view of his head between my thighs. His tongue strokes me softly, and even closed, his eyes are still smoking. I want to tattoo this image onto the back of my eyelids and burn it onto my brain.

My eyes are drawn across the length of his body, and I continue to gorge on the sight of him. He's fully erect with beads of moisture dripping from his tip.

I want it. My mouth waters, but it's my hand that reaches for it. Stretching sideways, I grab the base and stroke him. He hisses but in a very good way, so I do it again. His tongue starts darting into me again, and I'm overcome with jealousy. I pull myself sidelong, and he adjusts with me, until my lips reach the head of his cock, and I suck the tip. His hips buck. I drag my tongue along the shaft, but it's an awkward angle, and I can't quite reach the length of him.

He must have the same thought, because he rises, moving me underneath him. He's a table. I'm a chair. The six to his nine.

With full and unfettered access, my lips slide up around his cock, my tongue gliding along the silk of his skin. His hips give a little jerk, and he groans right into me, little vibrations fluttering deep. A match strikes. I want him to feel what I'm feeling.

I take him deeper into my mouth and suck until my cheeks hollow out. He sucks back, and I gasp. Another match.

He wraps an arm around the back of my thigh and slides a finger into me, then another. He licks and licks.

My head bobs up and down, sucking and sliding over his cock. My movements grow more desperate and frantic along with my growing need to give back to him the same exquisite pleasure he's giving me.

His hips rock too fast, and he slides out of my mouth. With both hands, I grab his ass and pull him to me. The tip hits the back of my throat, I gag, and he groans deeply. His back rounds until his mouth is pressing into my belly. He bites.

There's a brief sting as his teeth clamp onto my flesh. A thousand matches strike at once.

I am ablaze.

He grips my thighs so tight that I know I'll be bruised tomorrow, and all I want is to keep going.

He pulls his hips back until his cock hangs in the air above me. In a thick voice that's almost a beg, he tells me what he wants. "Squeeze your tits together." I do it gladly, eagerly, and he slides his length into my cleavage with a guttural moan. He takes several quick strokes, his body tensing more with each one until he unravels. With a spasm of small jerks, I feel him come in spurts and shudders all over my belly.

He tumbles to the side and collapses next to me. "I want to eat you alive, woman." It's both a groan and a lustful promise.

I'm startled by a quick swipe of cloth over my stomach before I see my white t-shirt go sailing across the room.

"You used *my* shirt?" I grumble.

"I wasn't going to use mine," he says. "I don't know if you know this, but it's cashmere."

I snort and roll my eyes. "You might have mentioned it."

We take a moment to catch our breaths, but not nearly as long as I think we're going to. Samite is bigger and stronger by nature, but I'm still caught by surprise when he lifts me off the bed. He scoops his arm under me and tosses me upward, catching my hips in the air and landing them squarely on his face. I flop forward gracelessly onto his abdomen just as his tongue slides inside me. I let out a cry of surprise as my thighs clench around his head.

There's already a tremble building in me. He pulls out his tongue, and I'm momentarily devastated by emptiness, until I'm filled again by the thrusting of his fingers. His mouth finds my clit, and he sucks hard. My back rounds as an intense spasm seizes my body, and I'm blinded by little flashes of light. I bite. My teeth sink into his belly. I don't think about it; I don't even realize I'm doing it as my hips rock against his face. It's not until the last groan leaves me that I realize what I've done.

"Sorry," I gasp, bolting upright. I don't taste blood, so I haven't broken skin, despite how hard I bit down.

"For what?" he asks as we both move to untangle ourselves and sit upright. When I meet his eye, he's smiling, and I smile back, momentarily distracted by his beautiful face and his bottomless dark eyes. But then I reach out and touch the clearly visible imprint of my teeth on his lower abdomen. He reaches out and brushes the imprint of his teeth on mine. "I think we're square."

His touch is light, and I've already come a few times, and yet I respond so quickly, flushing hot all over. My hips rise, and I have to bite my lip to stop myself from begging him to fuck me, to thrust deep inside me. I want it more than anything. I want it so badly that I'm shaking, so deeply that it cries out from my bones. But there's a line in the sand, a limit he set the other night, and I won't ask him to cross it. I barely hold myself in check, panting in frustration. It's the best I can do.

His hand moves from my belly to cup the ache between my legs, as his other one glides to the back of my neck and draws my face to his.

I realize this is our first kiss a split second before our lips meet. I expect it to be rough and fiery, but there's a tentative gentleness to the way his lips press softly to mine. His head dips to one side. The kiss deepens, sweetly, tenderly. He licks lightly at my bottom lip and when I open, his tongue enters with the politeness of a gentleman, greeting mine with a glide and a press that feels almost like affection. I melt.

He pulls back and nuzzles his head against my shoulder, hand still cupped between my legs. "My left horn for a condom," he mutters, and I can feel his longing as clearly and sharply as my own, but my heart leaps at his words, music to my ears.

I scoot across the bed and open the bedside table drawer. Turning back, I hesitate only a moment before I toss him the box. "Merry Christmas."

Chapter 8

Samite

I'm standing between Sofia's spread legs, rolling on a condom. I take my time because the way this woman pants and flushes all over is the fucking sexiest thing I've ever seen. If I was worried about her imprinting on me before, I'm far past that now. This moment, this memory, has already tunneled deep into my brain. It's mine forever.

Her tits heave, and her hips roll as she stares into my eyes. She likes the smoke. A lot. She's saturated the air with her excitement.

A dark instinct rises in me.

I rest my hands on her thighs and lean over her. Her eyes flutter. "Fuck me," she says, a demand steeped in desperation. It's her want, her desperate need, that's lit up my demon instinct. I want her as badly as she wants me, but she's closer to the edge. I have the upper hand, and there's an inner imperative I can't ignore. I must take advantage of the situation.

"Sofia, do you want my cock?" I ask, as if I don't already know, but establishing interest is a necessary step before I proceed.□

"Yes," she nods vigorously. I lean further, a knee resting on the mattress, and touch a soft kiss against the side of her neck.

"I want your entire body in exchange." It's my opening offer, and with that, our bargaining has begun.□

"You can do anything you want with me," she says. Mmm, I like the sound of that, but it's not enough.

"I want you to say it's mine."

"What's yours?"

"Your body, all of it. Say it's mine."

"What does that mean?" Her eyes are unfocused, clouded with lust, and her hands rise to stroke my chest. She's barely listening. Even better. The advantage is all mine.

"It's the deal on the table: my cock for your entire body." A deal that's highly in my favor, the best kind. An ancient fire dances to an ever-quickening drum beat in my mind. My pulse rises to match it even as my hips strain towards her. I grip the sheets, fighting against my own burning desire to sink into her. Our bodies are so close, already aligned, but

I crave the added euphoria of striking this *devil's bargain*, and for that, I have to hear the desperate soul agree to my self-favoring terms. She has to say it.

She meets my eye. "My body is yours if you fuck me right now. Fuck me hard."

Deal.

I plant my feet on the floor, grab her with both hands, palms flat against her ribs, and I thrust deep. She lets out a strangled noise of pure erotic delight, and I go wild. I pump in and out of her with little control, the intensity of my pleasure building like a volcano. There's lava in my veins and seismic tremors beneath my feet. But I want her to erupt first, so I slip one hand between her legs and stroke her with my thumb.

Smoke pours from my eyes, and she comes. She cries out as her back arches off the bed, her walls squeeze, and Holy Dark Mother Below, I swear I leave my body on my own release. My hips jerk, my toes curl, and I'm floating off the ground, swallowed by an electric storm that peppers my body with stinging, burning elation before I come crashing down.

My knees buckle, and I thud to the floor, my head flopping forward onto Sofia's stomach.

"Oof," she grunts under me.

"Did I hurt you?" My head pops up, and my heart stops when I see the dark markings across her rib cage, right over her burn scars, exactly where I held onto her. It's a pattern I know only too well.

"What is that?" Sofia asks. She's propped herself up on her elbows and is surveying her own torso. With a quick tongue flick, I taste the air. She's not afraid. Not yet.

"It's . . . it's my firemark," I say on a shaky breath. "Does it hurt?" I ask.

"No," she shakes her head, and I'm relieved. Fires created by demon magic always leave a mark and, like a fingerprint, each mark is unique to its demon. This one is mine. "Will it go away?" she asks.

"I don't know." I've never left a mark without a fire, and I've never marked a person. I've never heard of it happening. My mind runs a few laps, and finding nothing else, it circles in on an unlikely explanation.

The bargain.

There's an old wives' tale I vaguely recall, something about Mother Darkness adding her own bit of mischief magic to every devil's bargain, and I have to admit, this one felt different, punched up and particularly potent. But mischief magic is a children's story, and this has to have been a fluke.

"I can barely feel it. I bet it'll go away," she dismisses the mark, and pulls my mouth to hers. Our tongues meet, and soon we're burning again.

We fuck the night away.

After the measly three condoms are spent, I come on her tits again. She wants up on my shoulders to ride my face like we did in the kitchen, and I scoop her up onto my shoulders. She grabs hold of my horns with a giddy noise that drives me wild. This time, I have to be seated on the bed because the ceiling is too low, but she enjoys the ride, nonetheless.

We both pass out a few times. I usually wake up first, ravenous for her, but every time I try to eat her out, she goes for my cock, and so we're locked in a sixty-nine more times than I can count. I've mostly dismissed this position. It's an easy punch line for too many jokes, a cliché, but now it seems like an elegant solution to a problem we keep running into. I want my mouth on her, and she wants hers on me, and neither of us wants to wait our turn.

By the time the morning comes, I'm missing her even when she's wrapped in my arms. My tongue and fingers have pleased her over and over, but my cock is jealous and full of longing. It wants inside her again. I nuzzle her neck and kiss her cheek. "Are you sure you don't have any more condoms?" I ask just before I jump out of bed.

I go for the nearest door, the one I've assumed is a closet. Maybe she didn't look everywhere.

"Don't!" she shouts, but it's too late. I've already pulled the door open.

Inside is a stacked washing machine and dryer. For a moment, I just look at them, confused. She said there was no machine. So what are these? Are they broken? Did she not know they were here?□

No. She knew. That's why she tried to stop me from seeing them.□

I turn to her for an explanation, but all she gives me is a sheepish grin. I've caught her in a lie.□

I almost laugh it off, but then I think back to when she told me I'd have to wash the towels by hand. She lied easily, and I was easily fooled. At the time, I didn't feel even the tiniest twinge of suspicion. But I do now. A dark cloud forms in my mind as I cycle through all the things she's told me. Things I've taken her word on. There's only one I was genuinely suspicious of from the start.

"There is a way off this mountain, isn't there?" I growl. Why did I ever believe her?

"There's not," she says firmly, but her eyes dart sideways. "But—"

"But?! But what?" So, she has been holding out on me.

"There's a CB radio in the shed out back. I remembered it on our walk back last night. I was going to tell you," she says, but why should I believe her now? "We could call the ranger station. It's closed over the holidays, but there's an emergency channel."

"If we call them, they'll clear the road?" I ask.

"No, that's the city's job. The park rangers don't have that kind of equipment, but they run search and rescue when tourists go missing. So, they must have some way to come and get you."

❧❧❧❧❧❧❧ ❧❧❧❧❧❧

We return from our trek out to the shed, and Sofia slides the dusty CB radio onto the kitchen island, pushing it in front of me. "Merry Christmas," she says, her tone dripping with snark.

"So, what? You just say that phrase every time you hand anyone anything on Christmas Day. Is that the whole tedious tradition?" I roll my eyes at her.

She glares back. Oh, she's mad at me? That's rich. On what grounds?

"I don't know how to use it," I say, crossing my arms.

"Oh, *¡pobrecito!* If you can't call, how are you going to get rescued? I guess you'll just have to stay here and break more of my shit."

Fine. She has some grounds. I might have stomped around and shouted quite a bit and possibly knocked over her bedside lamp. I also may have busted through the screen on her back door when I tried to kick it open so that I could keep stomping out to the shed. I didn't apologize for either, and I'm not going to.

"Are you going to call?" I wave a hand at the radio.

"That depends on what you're offering." She wants to bargain *now?* I obviously can't do this without her. My head snaps up, and I stare at her. This woman has unbelievably good devilry instincts, and it's caught me by surprise again.

"What do you want?" I ask cooly, ignoring the twitch of my cock, my mind already flooding with all the delicious things she might ask of me.

"A new bedside lamp."

A lamp? That catches me off guard and stings my ego. I know she's been enjoying our romps. I assumed she'd bargain for more of me. But fine. Whatever. "Done."

"*De acuerdo,*" she says, mimicking my tone, before she calls the station. She gets an immediate answer, but her first question annoys me.

"Hi, can you tell me if there's any other way down the mountain besides Last Hour Road?" The park ranger on the line says no. She asks again, and he confirms in no uncertain terms that it's the only road, and she thanks him while looking pointedly at me. "I came across a lost soul in the woods, and he needs to get back to his hotel on Mount BZB. Can you come get him?"

"Is he injured?"

"Are you injured?" she asks me.

"No," I snort. Clearly, I'm not. Why would she even ask me that?

"No. He's been whining quite a bit, on and off, ever since I found him, but he says he's not injured."

I growl at her.

"I'm sorry, ma'am, but if this isn't an emergency, he's going to have to wait it out until the city clears the road. I'm betting they'll get to it before the new year. Unless something else comes up, of course."

I grab the thingy with the button that she's talking into, and I shout, "I'm stranded on a mountain! How is this not an emergency?"

"Are you at risk of perishing due to lack of food, water, or shelter?"

"No."

"Then I can't call in state resources. I'm sorry, sir." I start swearing, and Sofia grabs the thingy back from me.

She spouts a slew of nice things that the man on the other end of the radio does not deserve. Then she asks him how his holiday is going, if he has kids, if his family is in town, and he answers all her questions. Her last comment is something snarky about uninvited guests. Again, she looks right at me while she says it. And the fucker chuckles.

"I'll tell you what, Sofia," Park Ranger Chad says because they're on a first-name basis now. "Why don't I try calling in a favor? The equipment manager at the Emberlight Resort owes me one. He might be able to lend me one of their snow machines to come get your guest. No promises he'll say yes, or that we could make it up there today, but I'd give it a shot if you want me to."

"Oh, would you?"

"Of course. Anything you need. I'm at your disposal."

"Thank you, Chad. I really appreciate it. You have a Merry Christmas."

"You too, Sofia. I'll be in touch as soon as I hear back. It was lovely talking to you."

Fucking Chad.

❧ ☙

She flips the switch on the CB radio and the electric hum and static crackle abruptly cut out. The absence of sound fills the cabin, ringing in my ears. I glance at her, and she's looking back at me, not glaring, just looking.

If *'lovely to talk to you'* Chad comes through, I'll be gone soon. That's the understanding that passes between us. Her brow creases ever so slightly, but the look in her eye softens until there's no trace of the irritation she was shooting at me just moments ago. I feel my own irritation draining away. But the feeling that replaces it is worse.

"They won't come today," I say. Chad implied that, but I feel compelled to establish it as an indisputable truth. Not today.

Sofia says nothing. "Right?" I need her to agree with me. Not today.

She holds my eye, but her lids flutter like she's blinking away an unpleasant thought. "They'll probably come to-morrow," she says and looks away.

The word 'tomorrow' settles with an uncomfortable weight on my chest. But it's not as bad as the word 'today'.

We stay by the radio, both of us watching it like it's a kettle about to boil. Park Ranger Chad will call us back as soon as he has an answer. How long do we have to wait?

The silence stretches.

"I'm sorry, Sofia." The words rush from my mouth, catching me off guard.

"For what?" she asks with a puzzled look.

"Your door." I glance over my shoulder towards the back door.

"It'll take two penny nails to fix. Don't worry about it." She waves her hand dismissively. "A corner of the screen popped loose. It's nothing."

"And your lamp. I'm sorry I broke it." I can hear the embarrassment creeping into my voice.

She grimaces and gives me a one-sided smile. "It's more my fault than yours. I've been telling myself to wind up the cord on that thing since I arrived. It was a trip hazard. I should have expected that my flailing, stomping demon would trip on it," she says with a laugh and a shrug, but my heart has stopped.

She said *my demon*. I'm not sure she caught it. But I did.

"Do I still get a new lamp?" she asks with a teasing half grin. It's a playful question, an attempt to lighten the mood, but that's not how I take it.

"Of course," I say, pouring conviction into my words. There's one thing she needs to understand about me. "I will never back out on a deal with you." Never.

Her grin fades, and I think I see a tiny tremble in her lower lip. "I know," she says with a nod. "Excuse me," she mumbles as she brushes her cheek and gets up to leave. But before she can make it out of the kitchen, the radio crackles to life.

It's Chad, and he has bad news.

"Hey Sofia, I know you were hoping to send your guest home asap, but unfortunately, the soonest they can lend us a vehicle is Tuesday. Not sure exactly what time, but as soon as they deliver it, we'll head up. You can expect us before noon."

Today is Sunday, and it's still morning. She thanks Chad profusely and hangs up.

Our eyes meet and she says exactly what I'm thinking. "We have two days." A part of me knows I should be upset by the delay, but I'm quite the opposite, and she looks as relieved as I feel.

"Grab some blankets and towels," she says. "I'll pack some food."

"Where are we going?" I ask, excitement sparking.

"It's a surprise." She shoots me a grin that lights up her whole face before she shoves away from the counter and starts dashing around the kitchen.

We have two days left.

Two amazing days.

⬥⬥⬥⬥⬥ ⬥⬥⬥⬥⬥

On Tuesday, a pair of park rangers come rumbling up the mountain in a bright yellow snowcat, riding along on enormous tracks that drive a hard line in the snow, a nonnegotiable end of my time here. It's time to go.

Lo and behold, one of the rangers is named Chad. I glare at the hornless human, but it doesn't stop him from greeting Sofia warmly, like they're old friends. They are not.

Chad flashes his square teeth and tips his brimmed hat at Sofia, wishing her a 'beautiful new year' before he saunters back to the snowcat. I can't deny how damn suave it looks, and my chest fills with jealous fury. Demons can't pull off cute hat tricks, and I think this prick knows it. I don't care that he's the reason this yellow snowmobile made it up the mountain to get me. I loathe him.

I duck my head as I climb into the vehicle. The door slams shut behind me, and I don't look back. I don't want to know if Sofia's standing there watching me leave or if she's already gone back inside. Either one will upset me, but for different reasons.

There is only one black bench seat, and it already has an occupant, a tiny blonde woman with splotchy, red-flushed cheeks and the fucking biggest brown eyes I've ever seen. If she weren't so obviously human, I'd call her a crossbreed between a fairy and an owl. Her lower lip trembles, her lashes flutter, and all of it is a strange contrast to the stacks and stacks of cash poking up out the top of her shirt.

I don't know what to make of her or her bra stuffed full of bills, so I ignore both. I slide onto the other half of the bench and turn to the window. If I had my phone, I could bury my face in the screen and pretend she wasn't there. Phones are so useful.

"We've got one more pickup!" The not-Chad park ranger shouts back at us over the sound of the engine just as the vehicle lurches forward.

It's a bumpy ride over uneven terrain, and in between the swaying and sudden drops, all I can think of is Sofia. I asked her to come with me just now, as the snowcat pulled to a stop in front of her cabin. I was filled with a momentary panic. I'd already asked for her number, but she said she'd gotten rid of her phone. I asked her to meet me in town so we could celebrate the end of the year together. She flatly refused, then tried to soften it by saying the roads probably wouldn't be open. That's when it sank in that this wasn't a small goodbye. An ache settled into the pit of my stomach. It hasn't let up since.

"Come with me." My hand cupped her cheek. The park rangers were waiting for me. I didn't care.

"To where, your hotel?" She laughed. "No. This is the end of our burn."

She'd said something like it before, and I still don't know what it means. *What does that mean?* Why does anything have to end?

We hit a bump and my already queasy stomach sloshes side to side. The bitty blonde gives a stifled sob, and I make the mistake of glancing her way.

"Do you live in Winter Bliss?" she asks quickly, attempting to hide her own unhappiness behind a polite smile.

"No," I growl. Personal questions, of course.

"I'm Holly," she offers me her dainty little hand. I try to pretend I don't see it, but I hear her little hiccup, and it's just—*fuck!* I sigh and shake her hand. It's cold. She doesn't have gloves, a jacket, or a hat. This mountain is positively rife with poorly outfitted women. I want to ask, "Who is taking care of you?", but it's none of my business. And since when do I care about humans? I don't. But if there is someone, they need to get their act together because they're clearly doing a shit job. She looks miserable.

"What's your name?" she asks. Thankfully, I'm spared from having to answer by the sudden stop. We've arrived at another quaint little cabin, but I bet there's no brick hearth inside this one. No giant kitchen island or sexy, steely-voiced chef to lay out on it. I hear an echo of Sofia moaning as she comes, and I have to fight the urge to jump out and run back to her.

The door on the snowcat opens, and another woman climbs into the cab. She's redheaded and amply curved, another would-be treat to look at if her lower lip wasn't as trembly as Holly's. At least she's not hiccupping. I press myself against the door, determined not to be sandwiched between these two. I'm miserable enough as it is.

The redhead squeezes into what can hardly be called a middle seat on the bench and turns right to Holly. They exchange names immediately, first and last, followed by their hometowns, where they were born and where their relatives live. I expect them to exchange photo I.D.s and mother's maiden names any minute.

"Were you also renting a cabin for the holidays?" Holly asks. The other woman, who I now unfortunately know is named Noelle, just shakes her head 'no.' She doesn't expound, thank every god in the pantheon, and a blissful silence stretches out for three whole minutes before it's broken by another tiny sob.

Damnit, Holly! It's not that long of a ride. Can't you keep it together for a measly ninety minutes? Do you see me sniffling in front of strangers over my aching heart? No.

Noelle responds in the most humanly human way possible, just peak-human. She wraps an arm around Holly's shoulder, patting and cooing, and here come the waterworks. Holly sobs and spills her guts, downloading like a free app.

I tune them out as best I can for the next hour, but a lot of it gets in. A lot. I sag against the window. My horns clank against the pane, and my stomach continues to pang as we thump along at fifteen miles per hour.□

Did it bother her at all to see me leave? I should have looked back. I regret it now.

I perk up ever so slightly when the conversation takes a turn towards commerce. "Oh, that sounds wonderful. I'll buy a ticket!" Holly says. Buying and selling? That's an appropriate exchange between strangers and a worthy distraction. I heartily approve.

I turn to see Holly pulling one of her stacks of cash from her shirt and another tumbles onto the floor. "Oops!" She says as she bends to scoop it up. I want to sneer at her for being so careless with her money, but I have no ground to stand on. It crumbles beneath my feet. *Harrumph.*□

Still, she shouldn't be pulling out wads of cash like that. She's bound to draw the wrong kind of attention. I should know.

Noelle is inexplicably hesitant to accept the bundle of bills Holly hands her. Is she trying to raise money or not? Just take it.□

Holly notices me eyeing them and leans her tiny blonde head around Noelle. "Would you like to support the library? She's raffling off a big prize," she says as she shoves the flier into my hand. Paper. Great. What does she expect me to do with this? Noelle pipes in that the winner will be announced at the Truthfire Festival, but they must be present to win, and for some reason, that captures my attention.

The Truthfire Festival? Suddenly, the flier in my hand isn't trash. I look it over. If I invest in raffle tickets, I'd have no choice but to stick around to see if my investment paid off, wouldn't I? And if she happens to make her way into town while I'm waiting to find out if I've won, it'd be nothing more than a coincidence. A fortuitous fluke. Nothing cringy or desperate about that.

"How much are tickets?" I ask.

"It's by donation, so whatever you feel like giving. Choose your price."

"That's a truly terrible idea," I say out loud. My whole face pinches at the sheer awfulness of this scheme. *Choose your price?* "You're basically starting negotiations at zero; you realize that, don't you?" I ask, pinning her with a hard look.

"What? No, I'm not."

"You are. You're saying I can pay as little as I want, throw a few cents at you, and I'd be entered to win. You're supposed to start high and give me room for a counteroffer. That's how bargaining works, and you want to strike a good bargain, don't you?"

She blinks at me like a little red bird. I'd hardly be surprised if she chirped. "That's not really the point."

"The correct answer is 'yes.' Everyone wants to strike the best bargain possible. Now, tell me you'll sell me a hundred raffle tickets for a thousand dollars," I tell her sternly.

"But that's so much." She sucks in a breath. I'm sure that's what Holly has already given her. If Noelle plays her cards right and drives a hard bargain, she just might make two grand on this ride down the mountain.

"Say it."

"I'll sell you a hundred tickets for—for a thousand dollars?" she says in a voice that's far too uncertain for a serious bargainer.

"Five hundred," I counter.

"Ok!" Her whole face lights up, and I don't know how, but the woman's hair seems to bounce even more. She only had to counter once to get me up to eight hundred, and if she'd stuck to her guns, I would have agreed to a thousand, but so be it. I'll give her five hundred.

"I don't have it on me, but I'm good for it," I say with a sigh and return to looking out my window.

"The pay app info is on the flier." She taps the paper in my hand.

The park rangers drop us near the fire station just off the town square. As soon as we climb out, I pull not-Chad park ranger aside. "I need a small bag," I say. He gives me a quizzical look, and I level a glare at him. "A good bag, about this big, with a clasp or a zipper. Nothing see-through."

He eyes my horns nervously before nodding. He comes back with a knapsack with the park ranger logo on it, probably his lunch sack.

"Woman," I say, walking up to Holly. Don't use people's names if you don't want to build rapport. It's a useful little trick. "You're going to get mugged if you go walking around with cash falling out of your top. Here." I hand the bity blonde the bag, and she beams at me. It's the sweetest, glowy-est face I've ever seen. It's such a small thing, the bag, and yet she's smiling like I'm a butterfly that's landed on her nose. If anyone ever does decide to take care of this woman properly, they sure as hell better like being showered with open, sunny affection. I roll my eyes and turn to walk away.

"Do you need a ride somewhere?" Noelle, the redheaded librarian, shouts after me. I stop. I do, actually. "I can borrow my uncle's car. He doesn't drive anymore," she says. Her hair is bouncing again, and because it's red, she's like a cheery little cartoon fire, practically demon catnip. I briefly wonder if I should warn her, so she knows to steer clear of them, but then I remind myself, yet again, that I do not care about humans.

"What will it cost me?" I ask.

"This bag." She points to Holly's bag with a grin. I got the bag for free, so it's an excellent deal.

"Could you drop me by the Emberlight Resort?" I ask.

"Of course!" The two women, who are now apparently good friends, walk my way. "I didn't catch your name," Noelle says, looking at me expectantly.

"Samite," I say, my mouth flat lining as I follow the pair down the sidewalk.

"Where are you visiting us from, Samite?" Noelle asks me over her shoulder, and I rub my eyes in irritation as too late I realize what the true cost of my 'free' ride is going to be.

Chapter 9
Sofia

Two days earlier

"Where are we going?" Samite asks with a wide grin, his sharp teeth flashing at me with excitement.

"It's a surprise." I grin back. I zip through the kitchen like a whirlwind on borrowed time. This burn isn't over. I have two days left, and I'm going out hot and bright.

We fill a couple of backpacks and head out, hiking north along the ridge. Shortly before we arrive at our destination, the telltale smell floating on the chilly winter air gives away my surprise. Samite takes a big sniff and his face lights up.□

"Is that sulfur?" he grins at me.□

I nod. Sulfur isn't a popular scent the world over, but it is used in soaps and candles marketed to demons, and I get it. The pungent aroma in small quantities can add complexity, rounding out a scent much the same way bitter herbs can balance a flavor.

"Behold, my private spa," I announce as we come into view of the travertine-terraced hot springs. It's a natural wonder, a hidden gem, and my chest puffs with pride as we both take in the view. The hazy afternoon sun streaming through the clouds lends a dappled sparkle to the limestone rocks mottled with minerally browns and creamy yellows. The water is a brilliant turquoise. Add to that the snowy woods backdrop and the steam rising off the water, and it's simply—

"Magnificent." Samite pronounces, plucking the word directly from my brain. "Why didn't they build the resort here? There's nothing half as beautiful on Mount BZB."

It's true. Mount BZB doesn't hold a candle to Mount Winter Bliss, but the developers had their reasons. "It's an active volcano, for one," I say. Not that lava flow is a real concern. The earliest demon settlers, through crafty engineering and a feat of elemental magic, created permanent channels for lava flow. In the hundred and fifty years since, the channels have never failed. Sure, the mountain still trembles during eruptions, but the chaos and violence is tempered. Mount Winter Bliss is a safe place that doesn't feel safe, and it's one of the things I've always loved about it.

"And the lack of ski slopes," I add. Tourists love skiing. And gambling. The resort was built on the right mountain for what it is and for who it's for.

Samite rushes ahead, stripping naked as he goes, and I laugh at the eager hop in his stride as he beelines to the biggest, deepest pool and jumps in with a giant splash.

I collect his clothes, which he's discarded in a very un-Samite-like fashion. I fold and drop them along with our bags on a rock the perfect distance away. Far enough from the springs to be dry, but not so far that it's covered in snow.

"It's glorious!" Samite shouts as he swims a backstroke across the spring, and I laugh again, warmth bubbling up in my chest like I'm one of the pools.

I strip off my clothes, then naked and covered in goose-flesh, I take a seat on the edge of the pool Samite's swimming in. I sink my legs into the steamy water and let out a gusty sigh. There is no texture on earth that can match the sublime silkiness of mineral-rich hot spring water. And the temperature? Delightful.

"Get in," Samite says.

I hesitate. "I usually soak in that pool." I point to a smaller, shallower pool a few tiers higher.

"What's wrong with this one?" he asks, floating on his back, smiling up at the sky.

"It's deep," I say.

"So?" He comes upright, treading water.

Ugh. He's going to make me say it. "I can't swim," I mumble.

"What?" He swims over to me, pushing himself between my legs, and sliding his steaming hands up my naked thighs. I stare at his hands, and I don't answer. "What did you say?" He squeezes.

I try to meet his eye, but my glance darts sideways, landing on the gold cuff on his ear. "I can't swim," I repeat, flushing slightly as my eyes drop back to my lap. I'm a grown woman. I should know how to swim, but I never learned.

"Oh." Samite pulls himself up out of the spring. "Next time we come, I'll teach you," he says. Next time? I stiffen at that. What next time? There's only one tiny thread tethering him here. The lamp. He would never go back on a bargain. But he doesn't have to deliver it in person, and once he's made good, *snip*. There will be nothing connecting us and no reason for him to come back.

He stands and offers me his hand. We walk over to my preferred pool.

"This is the best one," I say as we descend the natural stair steps that lead us down into chest-deep water. Its proximity to the source makes it extra hot, much hotter than the big pool. Samite notices the temperature and gives me another of his delighted smiles, the ones that seem to shoot straight into my heart.

"I'm melting," he says and gives a happy little groan as he sinks in up to his ears. Same.

We soak and sigh. Muscles I didn't know were tense release one by one until I'm boneless and weightless. Samite pulls my puddle towards his. It feels entirely natural for my legs to wrap around his waist and for his arms to wrap around my back. My head fits against his shoulder like we were made for this. Our bodies relax by another degree, and we fuse together.

He kisses my shoulder, and I nuzzle his neck, and for a while, we're too content for more than snuggling and soaking. The steam rises in billows around us and the clouds sail by overhead.

"Do you want to try floating?" Samite breaks the long silence.

"Hmmm?" I ask as I lift my head to look at him.

"It's the first thing they teach you when you're learning to swim. Unless you're born with a connection to water, trusting it to hold you up will feel very unnatural. It just takes a bit of courage to work through that. Do you want to give it a try?"

I'd rather just stay wrapped around you, I think to myself, but out loud, I agree. I'm not a coward, and don't want him remembering me as one when he leaves here.

He guides me with light touches and murmured instructions. I like the sound of them, and they distract me just enough that on my third attempt, I lean back, stretch out, and relax just enough. My hips don't sink, and I don't tip sideways. I'm doing it.

"Nicely done," he says and leans over to kiss me, a light brush on my lips. "Next time, I'll show you how to tread water." He says, and I start to sink.

⬥⬥⬥ ⬥⬥⬥

We finally get out and towel off, and I hand Samite his clothes. He notes the folded garments and tilting my chin up with his finger, gives me a deep kiss that sets my head spinning. "You're welcome," I say with a loopy grin.

As we walk back to the cabin, Samite slips his hand into mine and laces our fingers together. So much of his warmth travels through his touch that the heat of the pool stays with me the whole walk back. We're in a warm bubble that the evening chill cannot penetrate.

"I thought you'd be more upset about a two-day delay." I say, and I know there's a question in there somewhere, but even I'm not sure exactly what I'm asking.

"I thought so too," he answers, and if I had to describe his expression, I'd say he looks mildly perplexed. "As much as I need to get back, saying goodbye today was—" He trails off, squeezing my hand, and he's quiet for a while before he speaks again.

"While we were floating, I pictured myself walking into my hotel room to find my investment egg gone, and it didn't feel the way I thought it would. It would take years, maybe a decade to rebuild my business portfolio, but—" He shrugs. "I can't believe I'm saying this, but if my money *is* gone, it's not the end of the world. I'll earn it back some way or another. I've started small before. I can do it again. I might enjoy it, actually." He tugs my hand, pulling me to a stop.

"Give me your number," he says. "I'll buy a new phone as soon as I get into town, and you'll be the first contact I add." He kisses my cheek before snuggling his nose at my temple.

"I don't have a phone."

He pulls back, and his eyes narrow. "The same way you don't have a washing machine?"

"No," I snort, wanting to be offended, but his suspicion is valid, and it's past time I apologized. "I'm sorry I lied about the washer, but you were annoying me, and I thought it was hilarious and served you right."

"That's not a great apology," he says.

"It's not," I admit, "but it might be the best one you're going to get." I tug on his hand to start us walking toward the cabin again.

"No phone," he muses.

"Nope." I got rid of it along with everything else, my apartment, my car, my self-respect. I even cut up my library card, and I love that place. It's a great big old building right in the center of town, and it has the cutest little reading nooks all throughout. I suppose I thought it was symbolic. I was cutting myself off from the town, but in hindsight, it was a needlessly dramatic gesture. If anything, I should be spending more time at the library now that I'm dead broke.

"What about the CB? Can I call you on that?" he asks.

"No. That's not how they work."

He keeps pushing, asking how the other residents keep in touch with the outside world, and I have to explain that there aren't many. Most of the cabins are rentals or occupied seasonally, not year-round, and those who come up here aren't trying to keep in touch. They come here to 'unplug'.

"They cut themselves off on purpose? Why?"

I shrug. Lots of reasons, but I don't feel like getting into them.

"I suppose if you're in the right company, the rest of the world doesn't matter," he says almost to himself. "But our problem remains," he adds with a frustrated grumble. I reply with a noncommittal wordless noise. He doesn't say anything else, and when I glance over, I can tell he's deep in thought. I like him like this. Like when he lost himself in the bonfire, something about being near him when he's pensive warms me deep inside. We walk the rest of the way in silence.

As soon as we arrive at the cabin, I head straight to the kitchen to start on dinner, but it's not long before Samite comes up behind me and starts kissing the side of my neck. His hands run over my hips, and it turns out neither of us are very hungry, not for food.

He picks me up and carries me to bed. I bounce as he drops me onto the mattress, but there's something in the way he's looking at me that tells me I shouldn't move. He undresses himself first as I watch, eating him up, my mouth watering.

Then he starts on me, undressing me slowly, kissing me all over with little pecks as he whispers dirty things against my skin about the places he wants to lick, about the parts of him he wants to put inside me. When I'm naked, not an inch of me hidden, he guides my body, turning me over and laying me face down on the bed. He kisses the nape of my neck. "You're so beautiful," he mumbles.

He works his way down my spine with more little kisses, inch by inch. His hands run over my back, my shoulders and arms, never pausing at any of my imperfections, and it's not long until my awareness of them is entirely gone. His nails rake lightly, sending tingles racing along my skin, and with every breath that leaves my body, I melt further into the bed.

When he reaches my hips, he palms both my ass cheeks, squeezing and kneading them like dough, before he leans in and bites. By the sting, I know there'll be a mark on the round of my ass, and I'm already looking forward to giving him a matching one.□

He spreads my cheeks and licks me and follows it with teasing little flicks of his tongue. My breath hitches. His hand dips between my legs, and I spread them wide, thinking he's going to sink a finger into me. But he goes for my clit. He rubs little circles over and around it. A shudder runs through my body, followed quickly by another.□

His fingers continue to rub steadily even as my hips start a gentle rock against his hand. His tongue licks again at my back door with longer and longer strokes. The shudders are coming closer together and little moans escape me, one after the other. I'm a quaking puddle, a jiggling gelatin.

His tongue prods, and I'm panting into the sheets, flushing head to toe. I'm right on the edge, my insides tightening even as my limbs are loose and useless. He circles his tongue, round and round my back entrance, matching the quickening motion of his fingers on my clit. Intensity peaks. My toes curl as my mouth pops open in a wordless groan, and that's it. I come undone, shuddering against the bed with delightful little spasms.

"You're so fucking sexy," he says with energy of a demon who's just getting started.

He abruptly lifts my hips, positioning me ass-up, face-down and a thrill runs right through me, followed by an aching need to be filled, and not with his tongue or fingers, which is where this is going, I'm certain. No. I want him pounding into me, growling and tugging my hair as he comes. But we're all out of condoms, and if I stay in this position a second longer, I'm going to beg him to fuck me without one. I don't mean a cute little beg, either. I'm on the verge of going full-on wanton temptress, wiggling my *concha* right in his face, and offering up my soul for the feel of his cock sinking into me. He just might give in, too, even if a part of him doesn't want to take the risk.

I flip over, rising to my knees, and I push him down. "It's my turn," I say.

He falls flat and stretches out on the bed, willingly toppled with an eager grin. I still owe him some teeth marks on his ass, but first I want to get those eyes smoking. I will never get enough of that.

He likes my tits on him. We'll start with some of that, maybe tease his balls a little.

"I'm going to play with you now," I say. "And when there's smoke pouring from those beautiful black eyes of yours, you're going to be good and flip over for me, so that I can bite that perfect ass."

"Yes, Chef."

When I wake up the next morning, light streams through the window. My head is on Samite's chest, and his arm is wrapped around my waist. We've gotten really good at snuggling, and I have to push away an upsetting thought about how empty this bed will feel without him.

I lift my head, and he greets me with a smile and a peck on the nose.

"Meet me in town for New Years," he says. "We'll go to the Truthfire Festival together. It'll be fun, and after, we'll figure out the phone thing." There's a glow about him that's more than just the morning sun, and a knot forms in my stomach. Until I have a new job, I can't afford a phone. There's nothing to figure out.

"I thought you were heading home for the holiday," I say, resting my head back on his chest.

"I want to see you again," he says, kissing the top of my head. "Don't you want to see me?" he asks, but it's not a real question because he's clearly not expecting a no. But that would be my answer. No, I don't want to see him again. What I want is to never stop seeing him. I don't want him to leave, but he has to, not just to find out what happened to his money but to get back to his fancy life and his business deals.

And me? I've got nothing. No job, no phone, no way to visit him, and no way to stay in touch. Six months ago, I was on my way up. I'd paid my dues in a brutally tough industry. I'd risen through the ranks, run kitchens for other chefs, and finally, finally I was getting my shot to unleash my own creative vision and prove what I could do. If he'd asked for my number then, I would have tattooed it on his body. But now? With no dream and no professional kitchen to attach my name to, what am I? Nothing.

Until I've figured out how to pick myself up from rock bottom, I'm just dead weight. No good to anyone. His life is too big. It would never fit inside this tiny, remote cabin that has somehow become my whole world. If he's thinking we can make this work, that we can somehow keep this going, he's wrong. The moment he leaves the mountain, this burn is over.

"You should stick to your plan and go home to be with your family." His body tenses under me. "The roads might not be clear by then anyway," I continue quickly. "I'll probably be stuck up here. It'd be better if you just go home."

I hear his intake of breath and know that he's going to argue with me. To stop him, I plant my mouth on his, sealing it with a kiss.

We spend the morning in each other's arms, or on each other's faces. "Is everything alright?" Samite asks me a few times.

"Perfect," I say and kiss him again. No need to talk when there's fuel left to burn. Hotter. Brighter.

"Slow down," he says. "We have time." But we don't. Our burn is coming to an end. Fire is magical but it doesn't last.

Tuesday arrives without me wanting it to. My heart aches so sharply it feels like I've cracked a rib.

"Come with me." Samite's hand cups my cheek, and I have to clamp down on a sob that's clawing at the back of my throat. I want to go with him.

"To where, your hotel?" I force a laugh. "No. This is the end of our burn."

"We've got to get a move on!" The park ranger yells, but Samite doesn't budge. He's searching my face.

"I don't understand—" he starts to say, but I cut him off.

"This is what you wanted. So, *ándale vete*. It's time to go." I give him a little shove.

He gives me one last confused look before he turns and walks away. He doesn't look back as he climbs into the snowcat.

They pull away, and at first, I don't realize I'm following. I walk along the tracks until the yellow cab disappears over a ridge far in the distance, and finally, I look around to see that I'm a half-mile from my cabin. I turn around and, hunching against the bitter cold, I head back alone.

Chapter 10
Samite

"**H**ow many brothers and sisters do you have?" Noelle asks me from the driver's seat of her uncle's car. I'm in the front passenger seat and obligated to answer because we've reached an agreement.

"Four. Do you know Sofia Moreno?" I ask. I'm sure she expected my question to be about her siblings in a tit-for-tat typical human exchange, but if I'm being forced to give up personal information, I'm getting useful information in return. I expect a yes or no answer. What I get is an effusive affirmative followed by a list of the last half dozen books Sofia checked out. As the town librarian, Noelle has no respect for privacy. I will never check out a book from her establishment.□

"Unfortunately, Sofia's a casual," Noelle concludes with a sad shake of her head.

"What's a casual?" I ask, my interest piqued.

"A casual reader. She has the potential to be an avid reader. I can feel it! She just hasn't met the right book yet, the one that will fan her spark into a flame and set her ablaze. Although, I'm pretty sure I've found it." She gives me a wink followed by a meaningful grin, and for a second, I think she means me, metaphorically of course. I'm the right book for Sofia. Something inside my chest swells at the thought. I picture us snuggled together in one of those reading nooks Noelle was going on about, but she destroys the image with what she says next.

"*Like Water For Chocolate!*"

"Oh, I love that book!" Holly says, jumping into the conversation from the back seat.□

"Good to know! Filed away," Noelle says, bopping her own nose before continuing. "It's an amazing story and the perfect book for Sofia for, oh gosh, just so many reasons. I've been holding it behind the desk for her. But it's been months, and I'll have to reshelve it if she doesn't come in soon. How do you know Sofia, Samite? Oh, I think her family has a cabin up on Mount Winter Bliss. *Oh!* Is that who you were visiting?" Every time she asks a question, her eyes light up and veer from the road. She asks a lot of questions, back-to-back, with zero pauses. But our agreement is one for one, not one for a dozen. So, I only answer her last question.

"Yes."

I might not have known I'd be visiting Sofia when I landed on her lake, but a five-day visit followed, so my one-word answer is true enough. My turn.

"Do you really think she'll like the book?" I don't know why that's what I ask. I suppose I'm genuinely curious despite the twinge of jealousy over Noelle knowing something about Sofia's tastes that I don't. Obviously, Sofia has friends and family who have known her for a lot longer than five days, but I can't shake the feeling that I should rank among the people who know her best.

New questions flood my mind, most of them personal and none of them my business, though I'm sure Noelle would tell me—How many friends does she have in town? Who exactly owns her family cabin? Why the hell hasn't anyone run a phone line up that damn mountain? I just want to talk to her. What year do they think this is, 1870?—but before I can ask any of them, Holly pops forward.

"You're thinking of sending it to her, aren't you, Sam?" She's scooted to the edge of her seat and her head is bobbing at my shoulder. "You should!" The little blonde pats my arm with eager encouragement.

"It's Samite." I correct her sternly. "Send her what? The book? How would I do that?"

"Noelle's fundraiser! Make a donation. Get a book delivered. It's perfect and so sweet!"

Hmmm. *Not a bad idea, Holly.* I glance at her but keep the thought to myself. The problem is I don't have a way to make a donation. My wallet, cash, credit cards, they're all gone. Although, there is my digital wallet.

"I need a new phone. I lost mine," I say.

Noelle whips the car around, and we head straight back into town, no questions asked, surprisingly. The detour further delays my return to the hotel, but so be it. I'll get there when I get there.￼

Getting a new phone with all my data ported over is unnervingly easy. Noelle is apparently best friends with the entire town. She knows the demon manning the front desk, but more importantly, he knows her. He's practically drooling over her red, bouncy hair, and because she vouches for me like we're old friends, I don't even have to pay for my new phone. The demon does as she asks and charges it to my account. This woman is a security risk through and through, and I make a mental note to switch providers as soon as I get home.

When we're back in Noelle's car, I make the donation to have the book delivered to Sofia. It's another of Noelle's library fundraising schemes, so again, the donation amount is 'any amount you want,' which is just mind-bogglingly ridiculous.⬚

"Will she know it's from me?" I ask.

"Of course! I'll be sure to tell her." Noelle grins, her red hair bouncing with her affirmative, and I have to admit, it's hard to look away from.

"Maybe you shouldn't," I say as a wave of uncertainty washes over me. I fiddle with my phone in my lap. We've never discussed books. Is this a weird gesture? A mistake?

"Trust me. She'll want to know it's from you," Holly chimes in with a reassuring smile. "Besides, it's important to show people how you feel, even when you're afraid they might not feel the same." How does she know that? I did not say anything like that out loud. "Actually, especially then," she adds softly, almost to herself, and settles back in her seat.

"And she'll get it today?" I ask Noelle.

"No, of course not. How would I get up there?" Noelle laughs. "I'll take it to her as soon as the road opens."

"Oh." I mull that over for a minute. I assumed she had a drone or something. She hand delivers books? That can't be efficient. "If I make another donation, will you deliver a bedside lamp along with the book?"

"A reading lamp and a book?" Noelle takes a hand off the steering wheel to cover her heart and both ladies audibly swoon. "That's a perfect gift. *Oh!* There's a pretty lamp in one of the reading nooks Sofia usually picks. She's commented on it before. Do you want me to take her that lamp?"

"Yes. How much?"

"Whatever you want to pay."

I roll my eyes. "How much did you pay for it?"

"I didn't. It's a family heirloom. My aunt, by marriage, got it from her mother, who brought it with her from Italy." Her finger darts one direction, then the other, then back again, which doesn't make sense chronologically or geographically.

"How much did her mother pay for it?"

"A thousand dollars!" Holly chimes in from the backseat.

"Good girl!" I give her an approving nod over my shoulder before turning back to Noelle to counter. "I'll give you six hundred."

"Seven hundred," Noelle says firmly.

"Deal." I start to extend my hand, meaning to shake her forearm, but before I can, Noelle squeals and stretches her hand back so Holly can gives her a loud-smacking high five. I snort a laugh. It's amusing how excited these two get over very small sums of money.

We make one more stop, and both ladies climb out of the car to join me on the sidewalk as I scratch my curiosity itch. The all-glass storefront gives us an unobstructed view of the gutted inside space. It's large with vaulted ceilings. There are no tables or chairs, only beautiful wall sconces, chandeliers, and at the center, a dramatic stone and steel hearth, easily ten times the size of the one in Sofia's cabin. A giant, shiny chrome hood hangs above it. As different as it is, it's easy to see that her cabin kitchen was a prototype for this. Her dream restaurant.

"Poor Sofia," Noelle says with a shake of her head, and I feel the same sadness echoing in my chest. "It's a shame it won't open. An all-flame restaurant? That would have been thematically perfect for our little volcano town. There was quite a bit of buzz around it, too, especially in the demon community. I heard a rumor that they were already booked a year out and another that Joycelon of Fire Division was going to be at the grand opening. It would have been something very special," she says with a regretful sigh.

"Restaurants are a bad investment," I say, stiffening and crossing my arms.

"Oh, I don't know about that." Noelle, standing at my elbow, tilts her head thoughtfully. "That's like saying fun is not a good investment. Sure, it might not make you rich, and it doesn't last forever, but imagine how sad life would be without any fun in it."

My brow twitches, and I start to chew the inside of my lip.

"Give me your phone, Sam," Holly says at my other elbow, and without thinking, I hand it to her. What just happened? I move to snatch it back, but she's already scurried forward.

She opens my camera and takes a picture of the 'for lease' sign in the window.

She hands it back and, with a tiny pat on my chest, she winks and says, "Just in case." What does that mean? In case of what?

I catch a flash of a plaid shirt out of the corner of my eye, and my head whips around. Sofia? My heart races excitedly until I get a better look at the passerby. It's not her. Not even close. Why would it be? She said she wouldn't come. My heart sinks again.

At Noelle's invitation, I have dinner with her and Holly because a demon's got to eat, and because Dark Mother help me, they're wonderful people to be around when your heart is in your stomach and your life is upended. The food they provide is unfortunate, but the company is a mix of silly and sympathetic, which is a good thing right now. They do that thing where they suck secrets out of my soul by listening too intently, and I end up telling them everything about my time spent on Mount Winter Bliss with Sofia, well, almost everything. Most critically, I tell them how confusing my departure was.

"Is she done with me?" I ask. They can't answer for Sofia, but *gah!* I have two human friends now. They make that very clear.

It's well past dark by the time I get to the hotel. "Good-night, Sam!" They shout in unison from the car window. I cringe at the nickname that seems to have stuck as I wave back.

When I reach my door, I enter the code and take a deep breath before walking in.

The bed is empty. I freeze.

It's gone. My money is gone. I don't know who ended up with it, but it's not here. I let out a sigh that's more like a painful groan, and my eyes squeeze shut.

Fuck.

I scrub my hands down my face and curse some more. But after swearing up a storm and slamming the door, there's nothing else for me to do, so I go take a shower.

I max out the hot water and walk in. The tiny shower in Sofia's cabin was far too small to fit both of us. We didn't even try. But this shower is three times the size, and it's easy to imagine her in here with me, her face steamy and flushed, her long black hair clinging to her neck and shoulders the way it did at the hot springs. I've been away from her less than a day, and I already ache to touch her again, to breathe her in once more. I inhale deeply, but it's only steam.

I lather up my soap, and the scent doesn't invigorate my senses the way it usually does. I turn on the extra jets, and instead of stimulating, I find them kind of annoying. I stand under the rain head and try to remember why showers are one of my favorite things, but all I can think about is Sofia. An echo plays at the back of my mind of her steely voice when she's in charge, and a delightful shudder runs through me.□

She barks orders. She bargains like she was born to it. And she cooks with some sort of unfair seduction magic.

Sofia Maria Moreno is part demon. If not through ancestry, then by the piece of me she's stolen. I lean back against the slick tile, and even with the stinging hot water raining down on me, I shiver.

From the shower, I slump onto the bed and fall backward, not bothering with a towel and not caring if the bed gets soggy. It doesn't matter. Nothing matters.

My head falls sideways, and something catches my eye. I pop up and crane my neck to look over the far edge of the bed, and there it is. My money, my investment egg! The bag is lying on the floor, toppled on one side, and the cash has spilled out, but unless someone pilfered a few stacks, it's all there!

I jump to my feet, unsure what to do, but I start moving anyway. I'm halfway through getting dressed when my phone chimes.

It's a text from my would-have-been business partner. If he's reaching back out to me, then things didn't go well with his other potential investors. Interesting.

$5M upon death, and I'll reconsider.

That's all his text says. Upon-death clauses are a modern interpretation of a ye olden demon tradition. In days long gone, if a demon had no money to bargain with, he could offer up something to transfer upon his death, his house, his clothes, his herd of goats, his wife. Anything. Regardless of when or how the demon died, the agreement was binding and had to be paid. It resulted in murder more often than not.

These days, an upon-death clause guarantees a one-way payout should a contract come to an untimely end for any reason. It's a contractual way to grovel. That's what he's asking me to do. Grovel and our deal is back on.

$5 million on top of my investment egg is more than I can afford at the moment, but not more than I can come up with if I liquidate my biggest personal assets. If I agree, and he voids the contract early, forcing me to pay out, I'll be homeless and bunking with one of my brothers for the foreseeable future.

On the other hand, if our contract is fulfilled, this will be the biggest deal I've ever struck. This will put me head and shoulders ahead of all four of my brothers and on par with my father.

I go brush my teeth. I come back to look at my money strewn about the floor. I go to the closet and get a fresh pair of socks and a pristinely clean pair of shoes, and again, I come back to look at the cash pile. I pace the room, then sit on the bed and consider it for a long moment before I scoop it back into the bag, shove the whole thing into the safe, lock it, and head out the door.

Chapter 11
Sofia

As the day stumbles along into evening and then night, the emptiness gets harder to ignore. There's a chill that I can't warm up from, but it's the echoes that get to me. I hear the sounds of him moving about the cabin, but they're not real. They're a trick in my mind.

I change for bed, and as I'm undressing, I pause to trace the outline of Samite's firemark over my rib cage. It feels strangely intimate to run my finger along the spiral pattern twisting with chaotic energy. It's my skin, but his mark. I'm touching both of us. I would keep it if I could, this connection to him, but it's already starting to fade, and I don't think it'll last.

I climb into bed and cuddle up to an embarrassment of sentimental nonsense. On Samite's side are all the blankets and towels he folded neatly and put away. I pulled them out as soon as I got back to the cabin and filled his empty side of the bed. I drape myself over the pile now and close my eyes, but it barely takes the edge off the aching awareness that he's gone.

Our burn ended. So, why does it feel like I'm laid out on a pyre?

I sleep poorly and wake up early. I can't sit still, so I hike down to Last Hour Road just before dawn only to see that it's still buried ten feet deep in snow. *Damn it.* I make the same hike the following morning, and the morning after, and many times in between. Anytime I hear a crack or crunch echoing up the mountain, I pull on my boots and rush out the door, but it's always a branch splitting or a snow pocket collapsing, never what I hope it is, a road crew clearing the way for me to get to Samite to tell him I made a mistake.

When I get back to the cabin, my teeth are chattering. To warm myself, I set logs on the brick hearth and light a fire. A cheery little flame will pull me out of my funk. My timer is set, I take a seat at the island and let my gaze soften into an unfocused stare.

He offered to stay in town through the new year. If I'd agreed to go with him, we'd be together right now. We could be holed up in his hotel, continuing our own mostly naked, and very steamy holiday.

My eyes bounce along with the flickers, but my spirit doesn't catch, and I get impatient waiting for it to happen. My attention lists, drawn to the window, and I find myself searching for signs of someone approaching. Do I expect him to scale the mountain to get back to me? No, of course not. Especially not after the heartless send-off I gave him, shoving him, and telling him to go.

What was I thinking? I should have ignored that damn cautionary voice in my head and let our burn continue through the new year. And after that? I don't know, but I'm sure I was too hasty in cutting things off. Regret is eating holes in me, and fire is the wrong thing to try to patch my-self up with. I tap impatiently to cancel the kitchen timer, and then I get up and douse the fire.

The next morning, I bolt awake at the sound of crashing followed by a steady rumble. They're here! I stumble across the cabin, bumping into furniture in my hurry to grab a coat and shoes and get outside. Even before I make it to the road, I catch glimpses of the road crew far below, working their way up the switchbacks. The noise of the machines and voices of the crew ricochet across the craggy, snowy moun-tain, and it fills me with giddiness. I squeal and bounce on my toes before turning and hopping all the way back to the cabin like a snowshoe rabbit.

But when I get there, I freeze. What's my game plan? Where will I go? His hotel? It's already New Year's Eve. Samite is probably long gone, home for the holidays, surrounded by his very rich family at their very luxurious home.￼

But what if he *hasn't* left? I pull open my lingerie drawer and grimace. So much cotton. I could forgo undergarments, but what about my closet full of plaid? If I'm going to show up at his door unannounced and desperate to see him, I have to be wearing something sexy, or I might just die of embarrassment, especially if he's not happy to see me, which is entirely possible.

Something sexy. I wrack my brain until a single option pops to mind, a beautiful outfit that is most definitely not plaid, but—*joder*. My stomach gives a queasy turn as I pull the garment bag from my closet. It's this or nothing.

The sun is sitting right on the horizon by the time the road crew gives the all clear. Hopping in my sister's car, I speed down the mountain, nearly colliding with a dark van headed in the other direction. It lays on its horn, and I brake too hard, fishtailing and skirting dangerously close to the cliff edge before I recover my steering. *¡Mierda!* That was close, but I can't slow down.

I take the farm-to-market loop to avoid town and head up the winding road of Mount BZB. It's about an hour's drive. When I reach the hotel, I rush to the front desk and ask for Samite.

"Last name?" The demon in a white suit asks, and I'm dumbfounded to only now realize that Samite never told me his last name, and I never asked. I try cajoling the desk attendant into calling his room, but he refuses. He won't confirm if he's still a guest, checked out, or if he has ever stepped foot in the hotel before. I get nothing. Samite would be pleased.

I climb back into my car and stare out into the dark night. I have two aunts and six cousins who work at this hotel, but the security is so tight, there's no way they could help me without losing their jobs.

Before I left the cabin, I assured myself he'd be here, that I wouldn't have to go anywhere near town to find him, but now it's the only place left to look.

My hands tremble as I start the car and put it into drive. I'm not speeding now. The car creeps along until I reach the fork, and my heart pounds as I steer right and drive past the sign welcoming me to Winter Bliss. "Have a *lava-ly* day!"

When I roll up to the first stoplight, my breath catches. The town is done up with banners, wrapped poles, and strings of lights. There are lanterns and torches, and seven-foot fire altars on every block, just waiting to be lit. It's every bit as beautiful as I knew it would be when I first suggested it.

"Let's open on New Year's Eve. It's thematically perfect. The town will be decked out with flame dancers and fire decorations. You have to see it, Ryan. It's incredible. And the volcano erupts at the stroke of midnight."

Just as I start to let my foot off the brake, a dark-haired man steps off the curb and smacks the hood of my car. I slam my foot back down, and my heart pounds in my chest. It's him. It's Ryan. I'd know that face, that hair, and that sneer anywhere.

"Watch it!"

I blink and it's no longer him. The stranger turns to grab the hand of a small boy as they cross the street. He turns once more to glare at me. Not Ryan. Just a stranger, but my heart is still racing and a cold sweat trickles down the back of my neck.

I shouldn't have come here. There's nothing in town for me. Nothing. A horn blares behind me. I step on the gas and take the next two lefts, heading back out of town. Tears prick my eyes as I retreat up the mountain, and I swallow the bitter realization that wherever Samite is, here or back home, I can't reach him.

The dark van I nearly collided with is parked outside my cabin when I arrive, only now I recognize it. I wonder what it's doing here as I head inside.

"Carlos?" It's my sister Lucia's husband, my brother-in-law.

He grins at me. "Hey, Sof! Surprise!"

"What's all this?" I ask. My first guess would have been that he was here to retrieve my sister's car, but that doesn't explain the massive screen he's mounted to the wall.□

"Your sister made a bargain with a demon and didn't get burned, ha!" He takes the time to laugh at his own joke before he explains. "This demon came by wanting to buy the cabin. He made a good offer, but Lucia refused. She wouldn't do you and the rest of the cousins like that, even though, you know, technically she could as the oldest and all." I roll my eyes. My sister's status as matriarch-in-waiting isn't an argument we need to get into right now. Thankfully, he drops it and continues with his story.□

Lucia and the demon struck a deal, and the short of it is, "We got all this high-tech shit. All we had to do was install it at the cabin as soon as the roads opened. Good deal, huh? I already set up the satellite dish outside. And this is a top-of-the-line video conferencing package: ninety-inch monitor, motion tracking camera, microphone, speakers." He points out each component. "It's meant for high-security, international calls, but you can also use it like a regular TV. Sweet, huh?"

"I don't understand." It has to be Samite, but—"How did Lucia meet this demon?"

"Through Noelle."

"The librarian?" That makes even less sense.

"Yep. Anyway, gotta scoot. We got the gig to work the opening ceremonies, and Lucia will be pissed if we're late. I still gotta get into my body paint and stilts." Carlos hands me what I assume is a remote and is out the door before I can ask him anything else.

The moment the door closes, the remote starts to ring in my hand like an old-fashioned telephone. I look it over, but there are no buttons. It's a smooth, featureless wand.

"Hello?" I say into one end of the wand.

It lights up a crimson red. "Hello. You are receiving an incoming call from a private number. Would you like to activate video conferencing?"

"Yes." My heart skips. It's him. It has to be.

"Would you like to apply filters to obscure your face and voice?"

"No," I say with a snorted laugh.

"Would you like to blur your background and disable location tracking?"

"No." It's then that I notice the logo at the bottom of the obnoxiously oversized monitor, a pentagon and padlock with the name Mammon Technology under it. This is definitely from Samite.

"Our recommended mode for all calls is full privacy. Are you sure you would like to accept this call with no privacy features enabled?"

"Just answer the call before he hangs up." I say with a huff, no longer amused.

"Your call will start in three, two, one."

The screen lights up, and I'm staring at his face blown up to a giant scale. It's like coming up for air, and I make a gasping noise I'm not proud of.

"Hello." Is all I can think to say.

I'm viewing his face in profile. He's looking off screen, probably driving, but the space around him is blurred out, so it's hard to say for sure. In the corner of the screen, a red-light flashes next to a string of aggressively red text that reads: private caller, data transfer disabled, recording disabled, tracking blocked.

"Good you're there," he says, still not looking at the screen. "I'm ten minutes out." He hangs up.

I have ten minutes to compose myself, and it's barely enough. He's here. He's coming back to me. My blood starts to spark when I hear the sound of tires crunching up the icy driveway, and I can't wait for him to knock on the door, so I rush out onto the porch.

He steps out of the car, and as he starts walking towards me, I eat up the sight of him dressed in an all-black suit. It's so well fitted that I'm struck with the same wonder I hear in his voice.

"Sweet Mother Darkness," he murmurs as he comes to a stop at the foot of the steps. "What are you wearing?" There's a look of awe as his eyes trace me up and down, and his face lights up with a delighted smile, my favorite of his smiles. I flush warm under his gaze, and when our eyes meet, a spark lights in my chest as surely as if he'd snapped his fingers.

"Do you like it?" I ask, biting my lip as I smile at him. This is the dress I would have worn tonight. After dinner service, I would have slipped into my hostess dress for the last few hours of our New Year's Eve party, the grand finale of our opening day celebration. It's clingy and metallic, low cut with sheer sleeves. It doesn't hide all my scars, but it shimmers like crystal in the moonlight, and the way Samite stares, I'm glad I didn't leave it hanging in the closet.

"I do. I like it a lot," he says, sounding a little breathless. Then he clears his throat and meets my eye. "I might like it too much. More than you want me to?" I catch the flash of uncertainty in his eyes and realize he's no longer talking about the dress. He holds his breath and searches my face as he awaits my answer.

"No." I shake my head. "I like it too much too." Way, way too much. The lines of his face soften as understanding passes between us, and I catch that lovely little flicker of orange in his eyes.

"I'm very glad to hear it," he says softly.

My eyes drop, and I notice he's holding a lamp. "Did you steal that from the library?" I ask with a surprised little laugh. It's a distinctive pattern of red and yellow Italian glass. Beautiful. I'd know that lamp anywhere.

"I bought it. I owed you a lamp, and Noelle seemed to think you'd like this one," he says. I blink as I process that.

"How exactly do you know the librarian?"

"We're friends," he says simply and, climbing the couple of steps, he offers me the lamp. I take it. It's not heavy, but the weight of our bargain adds its own heft, and it feels like it could anchor me in a storm. He followed through, just like I knew he would, but in a way I wouldn't have guessed. This is no mere replacement. It's so much more.

"Thank you," I say, looking up at him with a bit of wonder. How did I ever mistake him for anything less than incredible? His face is the most welcome sight I've ever seen, and as I stare, fuel is added to the fire burning inside me.

"Oh, and this." He pulls out a paperback book from inside his jacket but holds onto it with both hands, looking briefly uncertain before holding it out to me. "I read it. I think you'll like it."

"*Like Water For Chocolate*." I accept the book and read the title aloud. I've heard of it, but I haven't read it. I will now. "Thank you."

"It's due back to the library in three weeks but keep it however long you want. I'll pay the late fees."

"You're too generous," I say teasingly, but it's true. He's too generous. He's here. I can't believe he came back. "I'll return it on time. I promise. I thought you said you didn't own a jacket," I say with a wry grin as my eyes drop to his shoulders and slide along the line of his lapel.

"I said I don't own a winter coat. I don't need one. But I obviously need a blazer. How would I complete a perfect evening ensemble without one?" He dips his head, giving the impression of a bow. It draws a short laugh from me.

Gods, I've missed him. His particular mix of smugness and charm. There's a tightness in my chest, and it can only mean one thing. *Este demonio me robó el corazón.* This demon has stolen my heart.

"I was afraid you'd left," I say softly. I told him to go home, and the fear that he'd listened to me has haunted me ever since.

He takes a small step closer. "I couldn't leave. Not until I knew I had a way of getting ahold of you again." The flame dances inside me at his answer.

"You didn't owe me this. We didn't strike a bargain," I say, holding up the wand to the unreasonably large video conferencing screen.

"It's not yours. I made a deal with one of the other property owners. I owed her and was obligated to pay up." He gives me a crooked smile, and I laugh.

"That sounds like some crafty, underhanded devilry on your part."

"Thank you." He looks genuinely pleased, but then his expression changes, and he extends his hand in the small space between us. "Come with me into town."

"Why?" I ask. *We could just stay here*, I think, as my mind drifts towards the bedroom.

"Because tonight is a very special night. It's the most magical and sacred night of the year, and I want to spend it dancing and shouting in the streets with you. I want to kiss you, Sofia Maria Moreno, right as the volcano erupts."

It's a very good invitation, the best I've ever received, and I'd be an idiot many times over to turn this one down, but going into town? I already tried and failed at that tonight.

"Give me a minute," I say and head inside. I deposit the lamp, book, and wand on the coffee table and take a moment to feel my racing heart. It's nothing compared to the fire that burns beneath my skin. I am ablaze, alive with a flame that has me feeling opposite emotions at once: scared and brave, weak and powerful, uncertain and sure beyond any shadow of a doubt.

I don't care what tonight was *supposed* to be. I only care what it is now that Samite is here. It's New Year's Eve. I'm in a beautiful dress, and I have an invitation from a devastatingly handsome demon to the best party in the whole world. I don't care what reminders await me in town. I won't turn him down. Not again. I want this night with Samite far more than anything I want to avoid, and I'm going to have it. I grab my coat and walk back out the door.

He extends his hand once more.

"*Lista*," I say as I take it. "I'm ready."

⚘ ⚘

As midnight approaches, Samite pulls me to a stop. I'm covered in sweat, and my voice is raw from shouting. He has streamers tied to his horns, and he's lost his coat, tie, and shirt along the way. His torso is done up in body paint, courtesy of roving artists, and I've picked up my own festive adornments, a crown of gold glitter, strands of shiny red beads, and a sash tie-dyed like blue flame.

"Ten, nine—" As the crowd starts chanting the countdown, one of his hands slides into place at my lower back, and both mine loop around his, landing just above his pants.

"Eight, seven—" His free hand cups the side of my face, and his lovely black eyes stare into mine.

"Six, five—" I tug him closer as his thumb brushes my cheek.

"Four, three—" An orange glow flickers at the back of his eyes. I spy a wisp of smoke just before they close, and he dips his head towards mine.

"Two, one!" Our mouths meet in a tender and passionate kiss.

The ground shakes under our feet, and the crowd goes wild as Mount Winter Bliss roars to life. I can't see it, but

I can hear it, and I can feel it, the perfectly timed eruption that announces the start of a different kind of burn. A fire that needs no tending, no fuel, no kitchen timer to keep it in check.􏰀

We come up for air. He pulls me in tight at his side as we turn to watch the lava flow like destiny pouring out of the earth. Hot and bright, and timeless.

He kisses my temple.

This isn't a burn I could stop even if I wanted to. It's a river, and I can't swim. All I can do is let go and let it either consume me or carry me away.

Epilogue
Samite

S ofia has a place in town now, and when I come to visit, I stay with her. Whenever I offer to put us up at the resort, she turns me down and insists on her place. I like it when she's insistent. So, I offer her the resort every time.

But today, there's something else I want to offer her.

We're walking down the sidewalk, coming up on what would have been her restaurant, each of us carrying a bag of groceries. For the first few months, whenever I visited, we would detour to avoid this block, but now, no detour. I haven't asked, but I think she makes a point of walking past it every day even though it's out of the way to get to the mom-and-pop diner she's managing.

I grab her hand and pull us to a stop. "I'd like to open it with you," I say, turning to look into the windows. The space has been vacant for a year. No one has taken over the lease.

She grimaces, but then quickly laughs. "Aww, *que chulo*. That's sweet, but you don't gamble, remember? Especially on a restaurant." Her voice is light and teasing. She does that. She pretends like I'm joking when she doesn't want to have a serious conversation.

"It doesn't feel like a gamble," I say. I'm already invested in this woman up to my teeth. Not financially, of course. She hasn't opened that door yet, but in every other way, with everything else I have to give. So, why not my wallet too? Maybe she's right. Maybe it is a gamble, and if I lose, I'll lose big. But so be it. I've already pushed my stack of chips out to the middle of the table. I'm all in.

"You should try thinking about it with your head and not your heart and you might feel differently," she says, still teasing.

"I want to do this," I insist, but she's already shaking her head.

"Winter Bliss is too small to support a restaurant like this," she says, nodding her chin to the empty glass front.

"What makes you say that?"

"There was a feasibility study done," she says vaguely, and I'm guessing by the way her face pinches, she's avoiding mentioning Ryan. I've done my own very thorough homework, however, and I disagree. The realtor is over-charging for the square footage, but his hardline cracks a little more each time we talk. He'll come down. At a reduced rent, Winter Bliss could support the restaurant as long as the establishment ran twenty-four-hour service during peak tourist seasons. But I don't argue because there's another calculation I didn't think to make until now.

"Then open it in Chicago," I say.

"I don't live in Chicago."

"But I do."

She turns to look at me with one eyebrow raised. My heart skips in my chest. I've missed her face. I've missed her voice. I've missed everything about her, and every time I look at her, all I can think of is how hard it's going to be to leave her again. I don't know how many more times I can do this.

"Haven't you ever heard the saying 'you shouldn't mix business with pleasure'?"

"Who says that?" I snort.

"Everyone. It's a saying."

"Not demons. A demon would never say anything so obtuse." I shake my head and snort again. "How could anyone separate business and pleasure? Business *is* pleasure. It's a dumb saying."

"You're missing the point." She bumps me with her elbow.

"Enlighten me."

"If you have a personal relationship with someone and you add a business relationship, it doubles your risk. If either relationship goes south, they both do."

"Well, I don't feel the same way about risk as I used to," I say, hefting the grocery bag in a shrug. "And you'd like Chicago." I squeeze her hand. Her palm in mine fits like it belongs there.

"But would Chicago like me?" She asks and squeezes back.

"Oh, yes. I'm certain."

She laughs, but I'm not joking. There's a large demon enclave in Chicago, too, and a fire restaurant would be very popular, as would the salty, sexy chef who cooks like a she-devil trying to steal your soul. Not that I've done the research, not yet, but I will. I'll bring in outside experts to build a rock-solid case to convince her if I have to.

She tugs at my hand and starts us walking down the sidewalk.

"I thought you were in town to reopen negotiations with that mysterious partner of yours," she says. She likes referring to him as my 'mysterious partner' because I won't tell her his name. Why would I? She doesn't need to know, especially now, because—

"I've moved on," I say. We got past the upon-death clause. He finally dropped it, but even without it, a year is too long for a deal like that to sit on a shelf. It soured. I've invested in a few smaller opportunities instead, which leaves me with a sizeable chunk to play with. "And you should too."

"But I love Winter Bliss." I know she means it. I've come to love it, too, and not just because of her. I have friends here.

"We'll visit. You can keep your apartment, and we'll come back for the Truthfire Festival and any other time you want."

"You're serious, aren't you?" She says as she digs for her keys in her pocket and unlocks the door.

"I am."

She's quiet as she unpacks our groceries on the small kitchen island, and I can tell she's considering it. I grab a set of bowls and arrange them in size order. She drops produce into them, garlic, onions, tomatoes, peppers.

She pulls out a pan and a cutting board. I retrieve her knife roll and place it on the counter a second before she reaches for it. She starts chopping. "I can't afford two apartments," she says. It's a practical observation, not a 'no.' Hope leaps like a flame in my chest.

"You'd live with me in Chicago, and I can pay the rent on this place—" I say, but she starts to protest, "just until you start drawing a salary from the restaurant. Then you can take it back."

She purses her lips for a moment before she tilts her head and turns to the stove, lighting a burner. It's electric. No flame. I miss the cabin and the brick hearth, but not nearly as much as Sofia does. She never mentions it. She doesn't have to. This kitchen is at best half the size, far too small for a woman of her talents.

She pulls out a stone mortar and pestle and pounds ingredients into a thick paste which goes directly into a pot. As she continues cooking, I take the empty mortar, wash it and put it away, then clear the island and wipe it down until everything is back in its place, clean and tidy.

She's still thinking. My heart stutters nervously every time she looks my way. I've essentially asked her to move in with me. I didn't plan on it, but it's what I've done, and now there's no doubt in my mind that it's exactly what I want. Even more than the restaurant, I want Sofia in my life. I don't know what I'll do if she says no.

Sweet Mother Below, let her say yes.

"I'm over the French menu. I've been experimenting with some of my grandmother's recipes. I'm developing a Latin fusion menu," she says.

"Is that what we're having tonight?" I ask with an eager grin.

"It is," she smiles over her shoulder at me.

"And that's what you want for our restaurant menu?"

She hesitates, but then she nods. "It is." That's a yes! My chest expands and a grin spreads wide over my face, accompanied by a familiar tug in my pants.

"Sofia." I roll her name over my tongue as I walk around the counter, closing in on her.

She turns to face me. Her breath quickens, and I get the first faint hint of excitement in the air. So tasty.

"Turn off the stove," I say in a low growl against her ear. I want to rip her clothes off and lay her out on this tiny island so that I can devour every inch of her. She's mine.

"I can't. It has to simmer to develop a silky texture. If I cut the heat, it'll be ruined." Her eyes crinkle with worry even as her tongue darts out, wetting her lips.

My hands come to rest on her cheeks, cupping her face. My fingers curl into her hair as my thumb brushes the soft pout of her lower lip. "The perfect texture is a thing of beauty," I murmur just before dipping my head. My lips press lightly to hers, and she makes a soft little noise as I pull back.

"It is," she agrees with a trembling sigh. "I'll turn it to low and put on the lid." She turns back to the stove, and the moment she's accomplished her task, I snatch her up and throw her over my shoulder. She squeals and giggles, and at the sound of her delightful noises, I grow even harder.

"Island or bed?" I ask. I know which I want.

"Island," she says. "But first—" she trails off, and I know what she's asking for. She wants up on my shoulders to ride my face while holding onto my horns. I'm only too willing to oblige, but I can't pass up this opportunity to get something for myself.

"What are you offering in exchange?" I ask as I lay her down on the island and start unbuttoning her pants.

"What do you want?" she asks as she lifts her hips for me.

"That's not how this works," I say as I tug her pants down and off. I spread her bare legs to stand between them. "Make me an offer." I tug at the bottom of her shirt. She sits up, and I pull it over her head. I suck in a sharp breath through my teeth as I take her in, a wonder and a beauty. I run my fingers along her side where my firemark used to be. It's faded away completely.

"My body," she says, briefly biting her lip. "You can have it if you mark me again."

"I don't know how I did it the first time," I say, but I like the idea of trying. We'd struck a *devil's bargain*. She'd been panting with desperation, and I'd taken advantage of the situation. If it wasn't a fluke, let's see if I can do it again.

I reach behind her and release the clasp of her bra. It falls forward, and she whips it off and tosses it aside. I groan at the glorious sight of her round breasts and saluting nipples. I am happy beyond words to see them.

"Hello, friends," I say, saluting back. She laughs and starts to cover herself. "No." I swat her hands aside. "They like me. And I like them." I lean over and suck one into my mouth. She gasps. I suck harder, and she groans and squirms in her seat. I will work each and every one of her buttons until she's writhing and begging for more.

"Sofia, be still," I tell her. It's a tease because I know she can't. I move to her other nipple and suck it just as hard. She wriggles. "Don't move, be very still." I knead one breast and nip at the round of the other. Her hips roll towards me, and a tremble runs through her.

"Lay back," I tell her. She does, and I slide her panties down. They fall to the floor. She's naked. I drink her in for a moment, running my hands over her, down her neck, over her breasts and stomach, until I grab her thighs and throw them over my shoulders. "Grab on."

"Take off your clothes," she insists in that steely voice of hers, and I'm rock hard. Fuck, I've missed her. I strip quickly and return to her. I feel her grab onto my horns, and I hoist her up. She's panting already even before my mouth makes contact. I give her a little suck and then a light lick. She starts rocking, ready to ride, but with a firm grip, I hold her still. I continue my soft licks and give her a few little nuzzles. She tries to pump up and down, but I won't let her. She's not desperate enough yet. I prod my tongue at her entrance, but I don't sink in, even when she grinds against my face.

"More," she pleads. I lick from her entrance up to her nub, long and slow, but light. No pressure. And I do it over and over. She groans but mostly in frustration, pulling at my horns and pressing herself against my face. I stretch one hand further around and glide a finger, feather-light, up and down her crack as I continue the slow, soft licks.

"Samite, please." She's starting to beg. She's almost as desperate as she was that night. Almost. I prod at her entrance with my tongue and tap at her pucker with a finger, a rhythmic pulsing at each door, but no entry. I hold back.

A shudder runs through her body, and her heels press into my back. "More, I need more. Please!" That's what I want to hear.

"Say you're mine."

"Yes! My body, you can have it." I feel her vigorous nod.

"Not just your body. All of you, Sofia. You're mine. Say it."

"What does that mean?" She asks.

"I'm going to make you come screaming my name, and from that moment on, you belong to me. Deal?"

"Deal," she rocks her hips against my chin. It's as good as a handshake in my book.

I grab her ass, lifting her another few inches. I sink my tongue into her, and she groans. I start to thrust in and out, nuzzling my nose firmly against her nub between thrusts, and her breath comes faster.

At her back entrance, I work a finger a little way into her, just until I'm a knuckle deep and can feel the tremor run through her legs. I keep thrusting with my tongue as I draw back my hand to slap her bare ass. She cries out, and the taste of her excitement floods the air.

I slap her again, making a loud clap that I know has to sting before I wiggle my finger back inside her. Pressing my lips firmly around her nub, I suck. She kicks my back and screams as she comes, louder than she's ever come before. And it's my name she screams.

Fire magic tingles across both palms, the one groping her ass and the other holding her waist.

She's mine.

Acknowledgements

To Catrina for inviting Lark and me into your world, and to both Lark and Catrina for your friendship, support, and guidance as I entered the world of indie publishing. Thank you, *thank you* for everything. It is no exaggeration to say I couldn't have done this without you.

To the Winter Bliss beta readers, thank you doesn't feel like enough. Rosie, Trisha, Luna, Emily, Barb, Meagan, Amber, Melissa, May, Diana, Jessica, Mallory, Jenny, Peggy, and Jaime, you made *Holidays Ablaze* a better story with your insightful feedback. Extra thanks to Rosie and Luna for checking my Spanish and teaching me new curse words.

To the Winter Bliss ARC readers, thank you for reading. Thank you for reviewing and sharing. Thank you for all you do to build up indie authors and create a vibrant reader community.

A special thanks to the artists who brought the characters of Winter Bliss to life. Lana @redhead_trickster, Brina Boyle @artbybrina, Daniel Toro @dannotc_graphics, YArtxr @ylpha_artxr, and Sali @salisillustrations.

More Winter Bliss

Horned up for the Holidays is a series of three steamy, same-world, stand-alone novellas. If you've enjoyed *Holidays Ablaze*, please leave a review on your ebook retailer's website and share on social media. It's a huge help for an indie author.

- *My Indecent Valentine* by Lucy Limón – Sofia & Samite's story continues.

- *Holly's Unjolly Christmas* by Lark Green – Holly & Az's story.

- *Beastly & Bookish* by Catrina Bell - Noelle & Rom's story.

Merry Mischief

Merry Mischief is a whole new series in the same deliciously cozy Winter Bliss universe.

- *A Spark of Trouble* by Lucy Limón

Tropes: one night stand to lovers, black cat & golden retriever, he falls first

- ***A Court-Ordered* Romance by Lark Green**
Tropes: fake marriage, fish out of water, forced proximity

- ***A Frenemy in Need* by Catrina Bell**
Tropes: fighting as foreplay, second chance romance, only one horse

www.ingramcontent.com/pod-product-compliance
Lightning Source LLC
Chambersburg PA
CBHW030310160726
47992CB00005B/1956